Return of the Dope Boy

Sa'id Salaam

Published by Black Ink Publications, 2020.

RETURN OF THE DOPE BOY

First edition. April 12, 2020.

Written by Sa'id Salaam.

Prologue

"Well, what are you going to do now? Where will you go?" Killa asked through a dense cloud of smoke. The brief silence that followed gave hint to the answer that came.

"I'on know," Cam replied with a shrug. He had a new lease on life that allowed him to be able to go anywhere and do anything. Only problem was, he'd never really left his city and knew nothing more than being a dope boy.

"Well, whatever it is, you got a buck to do it with," his cousin replied, nodding to the satchel of cash he'd taken from the crooked cop. He certainly wouldn't need it where he was going. Hell is free; it's Heaven that costs.

"You sure you don't want any of it?" Cam asked once more. He wasn't used to anyone giving him anything so he felt funny about taking it.

"Nah, cuz. I'm skrate," Killa cracked and cracked up at his southern cousin's southern slang.

"I kinda wish I could come with," Big Shawn finally spoke up. Living in Atlanta, of course, he'd heard of the living legend sitting in his living room.

"Me, too!" Killa co-signed. He and Cameron had just met but it was obvious that they were cut from the same cloth. That fancy, sophisticated, durable, South Bronx denim.

"I wish y'all could, too," Cam sighed. The unknown that awaited him made him nervous. All he'd ever been was a dope boy. Could he be anything else?

Guess we'll find out.

Chapter 1

Cameron Forrest was dead but never felt so alive. The news had moved on to the next story the day after the bombing that had claimed his father's life. There was no time to mourn because it was time to move on. He had a new lease on life and intended to start a new life.

"Once a dope boy, always a dope boy," a sarcastic voice whispered. He realized that it was the devil, who was just doing his job.

"You's a lie," Cam laughed at the devil. The devil had talked him into more evil than he would ever admit, so anytime he won one against this rejected enemy, it was a big win.

Cam eased out of the motel and into his nondescript sedan. He'd once owned a watch that cost more than the car. He'd once owned cars that cost more than the hundred grand Killa had given him. It was every penny he had left so he held onto it dearly. Even he even put it in the passenger's seat beside him and fastened the seatbelt around it.

"Heads," Cam called as he flipped a coin in the air. It landed in his palm and he flipped it onto the back of his free hand. It came up tails, which meant he was headed west instead of north. That suited the southern boy just fine since he didn't like the snow nor the cold.

There was enough drama going on inside of his head that he didn't need the radio. Every mile marker he passed reminded him of something he was leaving behind.

A sharp hunger pain got his attention halfway through the state of Alabama. He strained his mind to recall the last thing he ate. He recalled that it was Britney's sweet vagina the night before and hit the turn signal to exit the highway.

He pulled into the first chicken spot he saw and ordered a three piece and a few biscuits. He thought about grabbing a room but shook it off. Birmingham was still too close to Atlanta so he took his meal on the road. The steering wheel was slick from grease as he multi-tasked.

Several small towns along the way invited him to spend the night with their motel signs but he ignored them all. He recalled seeing a sign for Longs, Mississippi and pulling off the highway into the sleepy town. The next day, he was on the run from another murder charge with young Cameisha along. He hated having to leave the crying girl behind, but knew that it was for the best. He knew that she was in good hands with his grandmother.

He glanced at the satellite phone Killa had given him to keep in touch. It calmed him and he kept on going.

Brrrr, the tires shouted as Cam drifted out of his lane. The Department of Transportation had installed minor speed bumps to awake drivers who drifted off to sleep and drifted off the highway. It scared the shit out of people but it beat the hell out of waking up dead.

"You right," he agreed and signaled to get off the highway somewhere in Arkansas. A trucker motel right off the highway got his attention.

It had the quick movement of drug and prostitute activity, which worked in his favor. They would draw all the attention while he got some much needed sleep. He pulled through the drive-thru check-in and got a room. The toothless clerk gave a gummy grin as she pointed him to his room.

"Hey!" two distinct voices attacked from different directions as soon as Cam stepped from the car. He gripped the handle of the bag tightly, hoping he wouldn't have to pull the pistol out of it. He snapped his head in both directions to assess the situation.

He relaxed, slightly, when he saw a young man coming from one direction and a skinny crack-stitute coming from the other. The teen's eyes darted around like a drug dealer's should while the woman's, on the other hand, had the soul-less look of the dead.

"Weed?" the kid asked, flashing a palm full of dime bags.

"Want your dick sucked?" the prostitute offered, also for a dime.

Not a bad deal for twenty bucks but Cam declined both. "I'm good," he said, shaking his head at both sleep aides. He was too tired for both so he went inside and closed the door. Once he locked it, he turned around and got a startle.

The room looked so much like the motel room in Mississippi where Cameisha had killed the old man that he actually glanced up to see if the clerk's brains were on the ceiling. He shook his head at the memory than cracked up at the memory of Cameisha and her Fat-Fat burger.

"I hope she get her burger one day," were his last words before sleep claimed his body and borrowed his soul.

****

Cam realized he was awake before actually opening his eyes. He lay perfectly still as he tried to get his bearings. His hand still clutched the bag of money, providing instant relief. His mind replayed the events that led up to this moment and he opened his eyes.

He rolled out of bed and headed to take a morning piss. The bag was still in his hand as he emptied his bladder. He almost took it in the shower with him but instead sat it right outside the tub.

"Nah," he told the dingy looking towel once he washed up. It had dried more genitals than he was comfortable with so he decided to drip dry.

He'd picked up the habit of watching the morning news from his dad. He had to settle for the midday news instead, thanks to the extended rest. A sense of relief swept through him when he didn't see his own face or hear his name. No one was looking for him but he was still on the run. Wherever he was wasn't where he was going so it was time to move on. He pulled his yesterday clothes back on and stepped outside.

"Want your dick sucked?" another prostitute asked as he blinked in the bright Sunshine.

"No," he said, despite nodding his head in agreement. It's just not right to keep turning down head. Besides, his body betrayed him. "You know what? Why not?"

The confused woman followed him back inside. He figured he could kill two birds with one stone by picking her brain about the area while getting some brains. That's like buy one, get one free.

She cocked her head curiously as he removed a condom and rolled it onto his flaccid dick. Only half of the tricks she tricked with used condoms when they had sex with her, but none of her blowjob customers ever did. She'd also intended to kill two birds with one stone. Getting money to get high as well as lunch. The condom meant that her stomach would have to stay empty, for now.

"Where are we?" he asked as she moved in to get to work.

"Huh?" she asked and took the latex covered cock into her mouth.

The warmth of her mouth made him decide that the question could wait. He watched as he grew hard and thick between her lips. It was obvious she'd once been pretty before turning her soul over to the drugs. Her thick crop of hair showed signs that it had once been well kept.

He shook his head wondering how she'd ended up in a motel room with a strange dick in her mouth. Thinking requires blood, so the blood from his erection moved north to his brain and he went limp once again.

"What's wrong?" she asked, inspecting his dick as if it had malfunctioned.

"Where are you from?" he wondered, twisting his lips in wonderment.

"Ferguson, Missouri. Just outside of Saint Louis," she replied with the perfect grammar of the educated. She caught it and tried to switch it up. "It where all da boogie folk stay."

"I see," he said, removing the condom. She looked disappointed when he tucked his penis back away.

"So, I don't get my money?" she whined and pouted.

"Sure," he said and gave her a twenty-dollar bill. He knew he couldn't save her by the look in her eyes. She would have to reach rock bottom first. Then, she could either bounce back or die.

Chapter 2

Once Cameron Forrest set his mind on something, he didn't stop until he got it done. He didn't pull off the highway again until a sign saying Ferguson, Missouri said that it was okay to.

He nodded in agreement with the working class city. It had the swift movement of the productive. People moved with a sense of purpose. Heads were held high from gainful employment. 'Good morning' accompanied smiles and waves. This was it.

An IHOP sign beckoned and Cam answered. It seemed like a lifetime ago since he'd eaten the greasy chicken. Chips, nutty bars and sodas had filled in since then but it was time for a sit-down meal.

"Paper, mister?" a kid asked as he rolled up on his bike. Had this been the hood, any hood, the kid would've been slinging dope or trying to rob somebody.

"Keep it," Cam said of the five-dollar bill he used to buy the paper with. The kid smiled so hard he couldn't get his thank you out. Cam heard it anyway and stepped inside.

"Booth or counter?" the hostess asked, seeing that he was alone. If he wanted to stay alone, he could take a booth. If not, he could join the debate at the counter. The regulars often indulged in animated debates over the topic of the day.

"Booth, please," he said, passing on company in favor of reading the paper. It was yet another trait picked up from his father.

"Being informed is priceless and only cost fiddy cent," his father used to say of the daily newspaper.

"You right about that," he told his father's memory.

"Mmp?" the hostess turned and asked as she led him to the booth.

"Mmp?" he replied since he wasn't aware he had spoken aloud. They both shrugged it off and arrived at the booth.

"The waitress will be right with you," she offered with a parting smile. She leaned in a little to give a little cleavage as she handed him a menu.

"Thanks," he said for both. He had just dug into the paper when the waitress came over.

"Good morning, what can I get you?" she asked with a smile in her voice and upon her face.

Cam began to reply before he even looked up from the paper. He was shocked not to see any violence on the front page. "Yes, I'll take... Oh my," he reeled when he looked up at the jet black beauty standing before him. His eyes shot down to her breasts without permission but hers were not on display. "Umm..."

"Your order?" she repeated, fighting off a smile at the tacit compliment. She had no use for men at this point in her life, but the woman in her appreciated being appreciated.

"What is your name?" Cam's mouth asked while his eyes read her name tag.

"Michelle," they both answered. "But I'm not on the menu," she added.

"Ca-Ca...um... Charles," he decided. A truck from Mercer Heating and Air passed by so he added that, too. "Charles Mercer. Please to meet you."

"Michelle, the waitress," she replied, covering her breasts with a menu. Not that the menu could cover the wonderful mounds of flesh she'd been blessed with. She didn't have hers on display like the other waitresses. Some well into their forties and fifties had left buttons undone. Perhaps for tips but Cam found her modesty even more attractive. While it may be true that you can catch more flies with sugar, they like shit even more. Something to think about.

Cam caught his composure and turned on his cool. He turned back to his paper and ordered, "Coffee, cream, two sugars. I'll be ready to order in a few."

"Sure," she agreed and turned to retrieve it. She just knew his eyes were glued to her ass as she left but she was wrong. A peek back showed his head buried back in the paper.

"Thanks," he blurted without even glancing up when she returned.

She'd braced herself for his flirts and come-ons but none came. Cam was too cool to sweat any woman. Besides, she was too square for his taste. He liked strippers and divas, not stuffy church ladies with their blouses buttoned up to their necks. Michelle was slightly confused by the drastic change in temperature. One minute he forgot his name and now he didn't even give her the time of day.

"Ready to order yet?" she asked softly when she returned to freshen his coffee. She actually used her normal soft voice instead of the terse one she used on most men.

"Two waffles, three eggs scrambled hard... bacon, and hash browns," he said, reading from the menu before turning his attention back to his paper.

"Anything else?" she sang, embarrassing herself.

"Orange juice," he replied and flipped the page. Cam fought not to get a gander at her ass as she walked away. He would have been impressed despite the loose skirt and stiff walk she employed to downplay those cheeks.

"Hmmph!" Michelle huffed in frustration as she reached the kitchen to place his order.

"What's wrong with you?" Michelle's co-waitress Sheila asked. "What, that fine man asked for your number?"

"Nothing!" she shot back since the truth didn't make any sense to her. She usually got upset when men pressed her but his ignoring her had her feeling some type of way.

"Tell you what, just give him my number and I'll handle him. Yes, ma'am, I shole will," she assured her. "Got them nice full lips, too! Chile..."

"Just nasty!" Michelle lamented when her friend detailed how she would ride his face like a bike. She was saved from more sordid details when his order came up.

"Thanks," Cameron said, flashing a faint smile when she placed his order in front of him.

"You're welcome," she said. She replied with a smile of her own but he had turned away before it could fully form on her lips. A sigh escaped as she turned to leave.

"Excuse me," he called before she left. "Can I ask you a question?"

"Sure!" she said eagerly. It was about time he asked her out or for her number. She would say no to both but still wanted to be asked. She was all woman after all.

"Is this place okay? Quiet? Safe?" he asked, pointing to an ad for a local apartment complex. "I'm relocating here and I need some place peaceful."

"Um..." Michelle replied, turning the paper to get a look. "Yes, these are nice! Expensive, too! I think a one bedroom cost a thousand-dollars a month!"

"I see," he said, reading into it. He assumed she couldn't be making much money if a thousand-dollars was a lot to her. He was on point since she only paid one-hundred-dollars a month for a three-bedroom house. Section 8 paid the rest and a portion of her utilities as well.

She waited for a few seconds to see if more conversation was to follow. He quickly filled his mouth with food to ensure none did. She put a slight sway in her hips just in case but once again, he didn't take the bait.

"Prolly gay!" Sheila offered when she returned. Women are quick to put a dick in a man's life if he doesn't pay them any attention. She'd seen that Cam had never looked up and made up her small mind.

"I...don't think so," Michelle responded. She'd clearly seen the attraction in his eyes when he'd first looked up at her. Then he'd turned it off so abruptly that he must have an on/off switch.

The two women watched him read and eat until his plates were clean.

"Here you go. Keep the change," Cam said when she brought his bill over. A twenty would have left a five-dollar tip that wouldn't hurt any.

"All of this?" she reeled when she saw it was a fifty-dollar bill.

"Yes, you deserve it. Thank you," he said, finally making eye contact. It only lasted a second before he was gone.

"Stuck, ain't cha?" Sheila teased when she came over to the now empty booth.

Michelle watched him walk out and drive away, still confused by the mysterious stranger.

Chapter 3

Cam let out a frustrated sigh as he entered yet another hotel room. This one was a lot cleaner, both inside and out. When he stepped out of his car, he was not met with offers of drugs or a blowjob as he made his way to his room. Being a dope boy, he was a veteran of many motel and hotel rooms, so knew to hold his breath as he entered the room.

"Okay, then." He nodded when he wasn't confronted by the violent odor of most motel rooms. Most contained a pungent smell that was a mixture of smoke, spilled beer, cum, blood, sweat and tears. This one, however, smelled of Febreze.

He sat down on the clean bed and contemplated whether he should take his shower before or after a nap. The nap won, so he leaned back and drifted away. It was nearly 8 am when he finally awoke the next morning.

He thought about heading back to the IHOP for breakfast but quickly shook the idea from his head. "She ain't even your type," he chided himself. She probably wasn't but the jet black woman had imprinted herself on his brain. He saw her smile the whole way to his destination where he was met by another one.

"Welcome to Westwood Manor! I'm Becky," a pretty white girl sang, flashing a pretty white smile while pointing to her nametag as proof. An older, brown-skinned woman who was sitting in the manager's office lifted her head from her computer screen to see who'd entered the leasing office. After a brief glance, she went back to her managerial duties.

"Good morning. I saw your ad and was interested in renting a one bedroom," Cam explained. He showed the ad as if he, too, needed proof of what he'd said.

"Sure! We have two left. Let me copy your ID and we can go look at one!" she cheered as if he'd just kicked a field goal.

"ID? I...um...forgot...lost...um...didn't bring it," he stammered while patting himself down.

"I'm sorry, our policy is..." Becky whined in sorrow at having to say no, a word she wasn't used to telling men often; especially not cute black guys like the one standing in front of her. He was older than her usual but cute none the less.

"Is everything okay?" the manager asked as she stepped out of her office as quickly as her tight skirt would allow.

Cam sized her up instantly. The push-up bra pushed her titties out of her tight shirt, giving a glimpse of a tattoo on her breast. The lace front, long lashes and bright nails had hood rat written all over them.

She quickly sized him as well. The slacks and button down shirt looked like they'd just come straight off a rack. They had. His clean fresh cut and shave didn't fool her, either. Dude still had the swag of a dope boy no matter how hard he tried to hide it. As the saying goes, game recognizes game.

"He doesn't have his ID," Becky moaned in despair. The poor girl only had two gears, happy and sad. Her boss always got a kick out of her.

"Yes, I left it back at the hotel. I can come back," he offered. He didn't have an ID but at least it would give him time to figure something out.

"No, that's fine. I'll take you to see the model myself," she suggested. "Becky, take my calls until I return."

"Okay, Gloria," she smiled and nodded, happy once more.

"Gloria Steele," she introduced, extending a freshly polished hand.

"Ca- Charles Mercer," he said, frustrated at the near slip. He could tell that she'd caught it and knew he had to work on it.

"You from The Lou?" she asked as she led the way out of the office. The model apartment wasn't far but she still intended to take the golf cart since she certainly hadn't spent all that money on her heels to be walking around in them.

"Excuse me?" he asked, looking up from her panty line that outlined her wide ass that shifted seductively under the skirt like a hypnotist's watch.

"Where are you from?" she turned and asked when his accent explained that he wasn't from St. Louis. Lots of dope boys from there went on the run to nearby Ferguson, but this one was from somewhere else.

"Um...California. Sunny San Francisco," he said.

"Okay, baby," she laughed at the obvious lie. His accent was Southern, not that funny California talk. They both silently agreed that he needed to work on his cover story.

The apartment looked even better in person than it did in the paper. The unit they used for showings overlooked the pool as a means to hook new renters. The view got even better as she led the way up the stairs. Her short skirt gave glimpses of her thick brown thighs as she ascended in front of him. He made the decision to fuck her so she would be Team Cam for life.

"Nice!" he exclaimed when they entered the staged model apartment. He would take this one just like it was if he could.

"It is. It's also a grand a month, plus a grand for security deposit," she explained.

"No problem," he nodded. He had no problem peeling off two-grand from the pile of cash. "What about the ID thing?"

"I ain't tryna get in yo bizness," she said, reverting to her native hood slang, "but my people in The Lou can hook you up. It ain't cheap but it's official."

"Not cheap, meaning?" Cam wanted to know. He once blew a hundred-grand in one weekend, but now he had no idea where his next dime was coming from.

"Like ten, plus one for me for the hook up. Like I said, though, it's official. Driver's license, birth certificate, passport, the whole nine!"

"Here," he said, digging into a pocket where he had a grand separated from the rest.

"Bet. The rest gotta be either a cashier's check or a money order. When you get your papers, come back. I'll hold a unit for you," Gloria explained as she scrolled through her contact list. She found the number she was looking for and gave it to him.

"So, what's up for tonight?" Cam flirted, ready to lock her in.

"Nothing. I'll be with my man. Holla at my people and then come back."

"That's what's up," he agreed with a nod.

They returned to the office so that he could get an application. Becky smiled and waved bye-bye like a toddler as he departed to go back to spend another night in a motel.

Chapter 4

Cam drove around early Sunday morning in search of breakfast. He put on a good show of contemplating and debating on which restaurant to eat at before finally pulling into the IHOP's parking lot.

"Newspaper?" a young kid asked as he stepped from his car. The youngster's hustle reminded him of him slinging sticks of reefer when he was that age.

"Sure," he said, eager to support his hustle. He generously parted with a five-dollar bill for the one-dollar paper. The grateful smile the kid flashed reminded Cam of his own children.

One of the downsides of being on the run is losing everyone close to you. It's either not see them at all or see them during weekend visits. If they really loved you, they'd rather not see you. They'd rather see you free than through prison glass.

Sheila smiled brightly when she saw Cam walk into the restaurant. She looked down to make sure that she had enough cleavage hanging out. After all, titties went great with waffles.

Cam requested to sit in the same section he had before in hopes of getting the same waitress as before, but it wasn't to be.

"Good morning, may I take your...order?" Sheila purred seductively down at Cam, who had his head buried in his newspaper.

"I..." he started to reply, but got stuck when he came eye to eye with mounds of plump titty meat. "Um... Is the other lady working today?"

"Un uh," she said, watching him scan the restaurant for her co-worker. Michelle was off and wouldn't be back until the next day, at which time she planned on bragging about bedding the handsome stranger. "She don't never work on Sunday. She takes her boys to church. She got two sons, you know. I ain't got no kids, but she got two."

"I see," Cam said and continued listening.

For the next hour and a half, Sheila told all she knew of her so-called friend's business. Sheila tried to cock block by painting Michelle as being hard to get while offering herself for the taking. He'd already had plenty of women like her in his life, however the modest, church going, single parent piqued his interest.

"So, I get off... at five," she said, insinuating she hoped to be getting *off* at five.

"That's nice," he said, politely declining her offer. She talked too much and he wasn't going to blow his chances with the black stallion over hitting this beige mutt on the side. No, he'd pass.

Cam ascertained that Michelle was a regular gal looking for, no, waiting on a regular guy to come along. Together they would live a regular life and have regular sex on a regular basis. That was right up Charles Mercer's alley. The dope boy just needed to find a regular job and become that regular guy.

****

"I could sell cars," he said aloud in response to the help wanted ad in the newspaper back at the hotel. "I sold plenty of dope. How different could it be?"

In the end, it wasn't regular enough and so he kept it moving. He probably would've been great at customer service, but shook his head at those openings as well. He was well into the Ps when something caught his attention.

"Produce manager?" he wondered as he googled it. He had taught his dope girl daughter plenty about men and the streets and in return, she'd made him computer literate.

Google led to YouTube where Cam learned all about the functions of a produce manager. He'd always loved his veggies so why not. Plus, being the manager meant not having to take orders. Hours of research made the time fly by until he was interrupted by his phone. Seeing that it was the number he'd called calling back, he quickly took the call.

"Hey, um... Gloria gave me this number. Said you could help me with some ID," he explained.

"Sho' you right. She told you the ticket, right?" he asked.

"Ten bands," Cam said quickly and listened for a pause. It would indicate that the price was lower and she was putting her own fee on top of it. Not that it mattered, since he had no choice.

"I'm 'bout to text you my email. Send you picture and the details. Just brang the money to Gloria and she got you."

"When?" he asked, wondering how long the process took.

"In the morning," the caller replied, since it didn't take long at all.

Cam agreed and hung up. It took several tries before he got a picture that he wanted on his identification. He decided to make himself a year younger when he gave his date of birth and to add an extra inch to his height.

****

Cam awoke bright and early the next morning to handle his business. The first order of business was to call the supermarket and set up an interview. Luckily, that too was on YouTube, so he just stuck to the script. With his audition set for Wednesday, he set off for Westwood Manor.

"Welcome to Westwood!" Becky cheered happily when Cam walked into the office. "You're back!"

"I am," he said, returning the smile. He shot a glance at her freckled cleavage and back to her face.

"You can come on back, Mr. Mercer," Gloria said from her office. Cam and Becky smiled and nodded at each other as he stepped into the office.

"Good morning," Cam greeted. He was actually enjoying being this new professional person.

"It is," she replied and shot a look at Becky who was still watching them. The look did the trick and she quickly turned her head to mind her business.

Once the coast was clear, she slid an envelope across her desk. Cam quickly dug into it to inspect the merchandise. His qualms about paying ten grand for false documents vanished in an instant. The birth certificate, driver's license, social security cards and passport were as real as could be. They all had also been entered into several databases that morning as well. Cameron Forrest was now Charles Mercer and could prove it.

"Here," he said, sliding an envelope of his own across the desk. It made the total almost thirteen grand that he would spend that week, once he parted with money orders for both his security deposit and first month's rent. Well worth it. Once Gloria went over the lease with Cam and he'd signed it, she called for Becky.

"Yes, ma'am?" she asked her while smiling at him.

"Walk 109 with Mr. Mercer. He just signed his lease,"

"Great! Sure!" she said happily and led the way. Cam locked in on her tight, young ass as she led him out of the office. The days of white girls not having any booty was long gone so he had plenty to look at.

The two hopped into the golf cart and rode it a few buildings away to Cam's new apartment.

"It's empty," Cam said, sounding disappointed when they entered his new apartment. For some odd reason, he'd expected it to look like the model unit. It was the same floorplan, just empty.

"Of course! Now you get to put your own stamp on it!" she replied, making it sound like the greatest thing in life.

"Put my stamp on the ass," Cam mumbled to himself when she bent over to pick a piece of paper off the carpet. She spun around and smiled, having heard him. "I'm sorry."

"Don't be," she assured him. Once she finished the walk through, she handed him his keys and her number.

Chapter 5

Cam drove away from the apartment complex with his head lifted in pride. He'd spotted a big-box department store the day prior and headed for it. It contained everything the bachelor needed to pad his new pad.

"First things first!" he said, rubbing his hands together greedily as he entered the electronics department. A sixty-inch flat screen showing Stephen Curry highlights sealed the deal. "I'll take it!"

He also purchased a state of the art smart DVD player equipped with Netflix, and quite a few other apps, so he could chill. Chill mode also required a stereo system with surround sound and a huge remote.

His next stop was the furniture section where he paused at a leather living room set that was on display. He nodded at the nice staging and bought it all. The sofa, loveseat, side chair, tables, lamps and rugs. He did the same thing with one of the bedroom displays. The kitchen aisle had a complete set up of pots, pans, flatware, silverware and glasses all in one big ass box so he grabbed one. He found a similar set up down the bathroom aisle and copped that, too. In the men's section, he copied the regular clothes off of the mannequins. They all looked pretty square to him, but that was the look he was going for.

All in all, he dropped another twelve-grand. It was a good thing he had a job interview in a couple of days.

****

Cam looked the part of a produce manager when he showed up for his interview at Cooks Supermarket. The fancy chain store was the Midwest's answer to Publix out east. The food cost a little more due to the fancy atmosphere, but it was money well spent to shop in comfort.

"I'm impressed!" the store manager, Mr. Waters, cheered after reviewing Cam's made up qualifications.

"Why, thank you," Cam replied. He was just as impressed with himself for his acting skills. It came so naturally that he wondered if he shouldn't take his talents to Hollywood.

"Can you start Monday? At forty K?" Mr. Waters asked hopefully. Cam recalled not only making forty-thousand dollars in one day but also blowing that much in one night by tricking in the strip club. Popping bottles and making it rain in the VIP while five women took turns blowing him like he was a wine tasting.

"Sure, thank you," he agreed with a firm handshake and eye contact. He had the job and that was cause for celebration.

****

"Well, hello there!" Becky greeted when Cam entered the outdoor patio area of a trendy taco spot. She wrapped him in a tight hug that caught him totally off guard.

"Um...hey," he replied and broke off the hug quickly so she couldn't feel the instant erection she'd given him. He'd gotten so hard so quickly that his vision blurred.

"Are you okay?" she asked fearfully, seeing his distress.

"Yeah, I'm cool," he replied as his cool came back to him. He flashed that brilliant dope boy smile as they were seated.

"You have to try the pulled pork taco! It's to die for!"

"Sounds good to me," he agreed. After all those months of no pork and no grits in New York, he was eager for both. He didn't see grits on the menu so he ordered pulled pork for two and two pitchers of margaritas.

"I think my boss likes you!" Becky blurted in the midst of their casual small talk.

"What makes you think that?" Cam wondered. He didn't get that feel at all from her.

"I'on know. I guess cuz she handled your lease personally. She never does that," she said.

"Oh, yeah, well... A friend of hers referred me, so she...uh...took care of me," Cam said to deflect things. "Besides, doesn't she have a boyfriend?"

"Keith? He's disgusting!" she reeled. She recalled the man staring at her breasts and crotch when he came by the office to take Gloria to lunch. "I'm pretty sure he's a dope boy!"

"What makes you think that?" Cam asked, knowing she would tell all she knew about the man.

By the time she gave up all she knew about Keith and Gloria, the pulled pork and margaritas were gone. No, there was no doubt about it. He was a dope boy for sure. A smart one at that since he owned several legit businesses, including a happening nightclub in St. Louis.

"So, what now?" Cam asked once the bill was paid.

"You got Netflix?" she replied.

He replied yes and led the way to his car.

Cam didn't want there to be any misunderstandings as to what he expected so as soon as they got moving, he reached over between Becky's legs. She parted her thick, tanned thighs, allowing him access to the pink treasure hidden behind black panties.

"Wow," escaped his mouth when his finger slipped inside her slippery box.

"Mmm," Becky moaned and squeezed his finger. She then turned sideways in the front seat and tossed one leg behind his headrest and the other on the dash. Next, she grabbed his wrist with both hands and proceeded to slam his finger in and her wetness as she thrust her hips.

It was no surprise when she came, but Cam was awed when she squirted in his hand. She thrashed around in her seat as her vagina contracted around his middle finger. He mashed on the gas and sped towards Westwood Manor. The speed bumps got ignored in his rush to get inside the girl.

They had barely gotten inside the door when Becky dropped to her knees and snatched Cam's raging hard on from his pants. His own

knees buckled when he felt her hot mouth engulf him. This wasn't or-
dinary head. This was white girl head! The stuff of legends.

"I'm...ugh!" was all Cam got out before exploding on her tonsils.
He was so excited from the action in the car that he didn't last two minutes in her mouth.

However, that was just the appetizer for them both. Cam pulled
her up and towards his bedroom. They both shed their clothing as they
went.

"Wow," Cam blurted once more as he admired Becky's fine, young
frame. Her heavy breasts were capped with large, mauve nipples. Below
was a hard, flat stomach above a strip of brown hair pointing to her
pussy.

"I second that!" she said, marveling at his thick dick.

He rolled a condom down and gave it two good strokes before join-
ing her on the bed. "Let's see..." Cam said as he used the remote control to adjust the bed. He lifted the bottom and lowered the top. Becky
flipped over; head down, ass up.

Cam couldn't help but to play in the pretty pussy for a few minutes.
It reminded him of when he was a kid working for Ali at the store. He
would crack open one of the girlie magazines and giggle at the white
girls. Now, it was no laughing matter. His dick throbbed to get his attention.

"Oh yeah, my bad," he told it and rubbed it against her outer lips.

"Quit playing!" Becky demanded and backed up to get him inside
of her.

Cam complied. He quit playing and proceeded to fuck the day-
lights out of her. In fact, the light of day had begun to creep across the
horizon by the time they wrapped up. By then, he had been in every
hole in her body.

"Can we do this again sometime?" Becky pleaded as she snuggled
up against him.

"Shawty, we can do this again all the time!"

Chapter 6

Cam spent a few nights rearranging Becky's box before taking Saturday off. He had plans for Sunday morning and needed a good night's sleep. There was no sleeping when Becky came by.

When the alarm sounded, he rolled out of the bed and hit the shower. Mainly to refresh himself before he got dressed. The suit he put on was nice but nowhere near as nice as the three-thousand dollar ones he'd left behind in his former life.

"Will the defendant rise," Cam joked at his reflection. The last time he wore a suit, he was in court facing manslaughter charges.

He strained his memory trying to remember the last time he'd gone to church. His mother's funeral so many years back came to mind. It seemed as if the only time he did go to church was for funerals. Friends', family and even foes'. It's not uncommon in the hood for the person who killed you, or had you killed, to attend your funeral. Nothing is as satisfying as seeing an enemy laying in a box. Once Cam had even told a foe to keep the money he owned him. Then he'd fucked his girl later that night. It's real in the field and he was a dope boy for real!

"Just wrong!" he laughed and shook his head at the memory.

Technically, wrong would be the intent behind him going to church today, if he was going just to get at what was between Michelle's legs. Yes, that would be wrong; dead wrong. But since he wanted the whole woman, he didn't see it as being bad. Actions are judged by the intent behind them. Everyone will have what they intended.

****

"Shit!" Cam exclaimed as he parked in the crowded church's parking lot. Not because of how crowded it was but because there was ass and cleavage as far as his eyes could see. So much so that he almost forgot about Michelle until he saw her get out of her old car.

24

She wore a tasteful dress that couldn't conceal the large mound of ass she toted. Black hose hugged her firm calf muscles above a two-inch pair of pumps. Two handsome boys followed her out of the car. The oldest looked to be about twelve and judging by his slight high water suit pants, he was growing faster than she could keep up with. The younger one was about seven and hadn't quite yet grown into the hand-me-down suit he'd gotten from his brother. Both appeared to be well-behaved compared to the ripping and running of the other boys. Someone was bound to get fucked up for fucking up their church clothes.

Cam had to sit and rest for a second before getting out of the car. All that ass and titties on display had given him a semi-erection. Can't go into church like that.

"And God-dah..." the preacher preached as Cam came in and scanned the congregation. Plenty of eyes found his and smiled flirtatiously. He was new meat, after all.

Cam spotted Michelle and took a seat a few pews behind her. He was close enough to keep an eye on her, yet far enough to avoid a stalking charge.

The preacher was really putting on and actually held Cam's attention. He believed in God, one God, but not much beyond that. Still, it was a good start. "Join me-ah for a song-ah!" the colorful preacher demanded. Everyone rose, like in court, and joined him in song. Cam didn't know the words so he lip-synced just so he could be down.

"Reminds me of a strip club," Cam mumbled when the collection plate came around for the third time. He wondered why they didn't just charge admission and get it all at once.

"Do we have-ah any visitors-ah to our flock-ah?" the pastor wanted to know as he brought the sermon to a close.

Cam had absolutely no intention on standing up to introduce himself but with so many faces turned to his, he felt compelled to do so. A long winded woman gave him time to come up with a story of his own while she told hers.

"Hello, I'm Charles, Charles Mercy...Mercer," he said with all eyes on him.

Michelle turned and went wide eyed at the sight of him.

"I'm just moving to town from California. My wife died a few years back and I needed a fresh start. A new life..." he explained. At the moment, he could have picked anyone of the hundred single sisters staring at him in awe. He was handsome, single, had a good job, and he was fresh meat.

Michelle smiled with a sense of ownership since she'd already met him before. She squinted at him to confirm that he was indeed the one. He damn sure looked like the one. When their eyes met, their souls synced and it was just a matter of time. After the service, they gravitated towards each other like magnets.

"You came to my restaurant," she reminded, just in case he'd forgotten.

"Yes, and you served me. Thank you," he said humbly. He noticed the boys staring curiously and introduced himself, "Hey, guys, I'm Charles."

"Hello, Mr. Charles," they greeted in unison.

"Nice to meet you guys. If your mom and dad don't mind, maybe we could go to the park someday and toss around a football?" he asked, looking to her for approval.

"Our dad is dead," the younger one explained, not knowing that Cam already knew.

****

The relationship between the two grew at a slow yet steady pace. Cam often took the family to dinner and the movies. On weekends, he and the boys would play sports and do guy stuff. Months had passed and he and Michelle had yet to shake hands.

Luckily, he still had Becky to take out his sexual frustrations on. Plenty of nights he left Michelle's to play inside the pretty white girl. They used each other, so no one was wronged.

A year later, Cam stood at the altar with young Brian by his side while the older Raymond walked their mom down the aisle. Her white dress looked stunning against her dark skin. Even hating ass Sheila couldn't deny that she was a beautiful bride.

"Do you-ah take-ah this woman-ah..." the preacher asked as he conducted the wedding ceremony. Cam fought the urge to shout *come the fuck on-ah* as he spoke.

"I do," he said and she co-signed and they were married. The wedding guests then retreated out back to eat the wedding feast.

Cam smiled graciously as he accepted congrats and envelopes with ten and twenty dollar gifts enclosed. He was genuinely happy enjoying his regular life with his regular wife. It finally dawned on him that he was no longer a dope boy.

"I'm taking the boys home with me," Sheila announced as she approached the bride and groom's table.

"Okay," Michelle replied since it was a statement, not a question. Besides, she appreciated that she wanted the newlyweds to have some privacy on their wedding night. A honeymoon wasn't in the budget, but they did have the weekend.

****

"Well, here we are," Cam said with a sigh when Michelle joined him on the bed. He'd abandoned the wildness of sex with Becky's vagina a month ago for what he expected to be a tame night of mild sex with his new wife.

"Yes, here we are," she replied with a smirk. She knew full well what the sigh was about. She knew that her new husband assumed that since she was a good, moral woman that the sex would be plain. Boy, was he in for a surprise. She was a freak once that ring was on her finger.

The couple leaned in and shared their first kiss. It was a tentative peck followed by another, and another, until Michelle upped the ante when she slipped her tongue inside his mouth.

"Mmm," she moaned as he sucked on her tongue and rubbed her leg. She parted her thick thighs, giving him access to her goodies just in case he wanted her to. He didn't. Not yet, anyway.

"Stand up, let me see you," he ordered, his voice thick with lust. She still had on the bathrobe she'd emerged from the bathroom in.

Michelle stood and let the robe fall open, causing Cam's dick to throb in appreciation. His eyes blinked rapidly trying to make sense of the white lace against her jet black skin while taking in her plump breasts that protruded from the confines of her bra urging to be set free.

"You like?" she asked as she did a slow spin to show off her ass hanging from beneath her French cut panties.

"I love you," he answered. He loved the whole woman, not just her body. "Come here, I'll be gentle."

"Don't," she replied and complied. She had been celibate in the five years since her husband was killed. Although Cam was curious, he still hadn't asked her about his murder.

Michelle reached behind her back and unhooked her bra, allowing her heavy, firm breasts to stand at attention. Shen then stepped out of her panties while Cam came out of his boxer briefs.

"Huh?" he wondered when she shoved him flat on is back.

The answer came when she turned around and swung a leg over his face before beginning her half of the sixty-nine with kisses atop his swollen dick head. He almost lost it when she immersed half of his shaft into her mouth. Michelle's vagina was so dark it looked purple, like a plum. And plums are good eating.

"Ssss," Michelle hissed when he clamped his mouth on her lips. She came instantly. Five years, after all, was a long time. His mouth filled with her plum's juices but he kept right on going.

She couldn't concentrate on her half of the sixty-nine with him sucking and slurping on her hot box. The best she could do was to stroke his shaft with her hand. Obviously, that was plenty since, with a grunt, he came, sending semen five feet in the air.

With the score tied at one nut apiece, it was now time to make love. Michelle switched places with her husband and extended an invitation to her insides by parting her thick thighs. Taking her up on her offer, Cam took position between her dark chocolate thighs and kissed her.

Michelle kissed, licked and sucked on his mouth and chin vigorously. One, because she loved him and two, because she loved the taste of her own juices, although she'd never admit it.

"Mmm," they purred and growled together as he sank slowly into her vagina. Her cervix signaled the end of the road. He grinded against it before slowly retreating to her opening then dipping back in again. Cam slid in and out with slow, methodical strokes that grew faster, deeper and harder until the sound of skin slapping echoed throughout the quiet room.

Michelle pulled her legs back to make sure he got it all. In return, Cam lifted up on his arms and made sure that he took it all. Cam came first, yet managed to hang in there while she grinded out a nut of her own.

"I love you," he sighed, meaning every letter of the words he spoke. She returned the sentiment with an 'I love you more' before drifting away into that good sleep that only a good nut can produce.

Cam felt the aftereffects of their good loving as well but his mind was too busy racing to sleep. How long could he keep up this charade? Would she still love him more if she found out that he was really a dope boy?

Chapter 7

Becky pouted like a spoiled kid when Cam came to turn his keys in. Her favorite toy was being taken away from her and she didn't like it one bit. Likewise, he avoided her green-eyed gaze, hoping not to fall into her pussy trap again. He was a married man now, just a regular guy with a regular life.

"You gone?" Gloria asked as she stepped from her office. It was purely rhetorical since he'd given notice. Cam was moving in with Michelle and the boys so he had no more use for the apartment. Once upon a time, it would have made a perfect stash spot. A low key place to keep drugs, money and side chicks.

"I'm gone," he replied, noticing stress on her face. It was none of his business but he still asked, "Is everything okay?"

"No, but I'll figure something out," she replied. It was none of his business but she still said, "Keith done got himself in some trouble."

"Oh," he replied. He really didn't care to know more and luckily she didn't say more.

Keith was more than just in trouble; he was in deep shit. A shipment of dope was knocked off by his careless workers. Dude was smoking a blunt while transporting fifty-bricks of pure cocaine. The Mexican Mafia did not take losing money lightly.

****

"Need some help, dad?" Brian asked as Cam headed into the backyard to tend to his garden. He found horticulture so fascinating that he started growing a crop of his own.

"Sure, son," he replied proudly. Cam sometimes felt guilty about being such a great stepdad while not being able to be in his own children's lives. The only thing that gave him solace was knowing he would one day return.

"I'll help, too!" Raymond insisted and rushed out behind them. The older Raymond still called him Mr. Charles but they were just as close.

Michelle watched proudly as her sons helped her husband out in the garden. She decided to cook him his favorite meal then fuck him real good when they went to bed. Her panties got wet with anticipation.

A strange sound rang out, interrupting her blissful daydream. She followed the sound to her room and saw it was her husband's phone. It was one of the mysteries of the mysterious man. He always kept charged, checked it often but she never saw him use it. Cam did use the phone from time to time to check on his grandmother and Cameisha in the Bronx. She knew it was important to him so she rushed to let him know.

"Charles! Charles, that phone is ringing! You know, the one in...the...room," she huffed out of breath form the sprint.

Cam froze as the strangest feeling swept over him. He couldn't identify what it was since he'd never felt fear before in his life. He didn't know he was stuck until his wife called him again.

"The phone, the other one," she said as if she shared in its secret.

"How long ago?" he wondered as its protocol came back to him. The Forrest family all kept satellite phones to keep in touch no matter where they may be. The high tech devices cost a pretty penny but were well worth it since they always had a signal.

"Just now," she replied since she didn't know about the five-minute rule. Whenever the need came to use one of the phones, the rule was you call every five minutes until you get an answer.

Cam let out a sigh and rushed inside. All kind of scenarios played in his mind as he rushed up the stairs. Five minutes were up and the phone began to ring again as soon as he reached it.

"Hello?" he asked instead of greeted, and then braced himself.

"Sup, cuz!" a voice smiled through the crystal clear line.

"Killa? Is grandma a'right?" he needed to know.

"Yeah, she good. The girl good. I'm good but... uh... What could you do with ten-thousand keys?"

"My bad," Cam replied once he picked up the dropped phone. "I...um...see, I...okay, look-it...I...um..."

Killa chuckled at his confused cousin as he scrambled for excuses. He personally didn't believe a tiger could change its stripes. Once a dope boy, always a dope boy.

Cam was still stammering and stuttering, grasping for excuses and reasons for not doing it, while one part of his brain reasoned to do it. He had run through all the money he'd inherited from the crooked cop. Forty-grand a year is a lot less after taxes and insurance. He had mouths to feed and was damn near living check to check after a year of marriage.

He caught a glimpse of his family in the backyard and wondered if it would help or hurt them. On the one hand, it would set them straight for life. Ten-thousand kilos at a clearance price of twenty-five thousand apiece would net two-and-half million. That would set them straight for life. However, on the other hand, if he failed, he would lose everything all over again. Once again, his family would lose its head. What would they do then?

"Bring it!" Cam decided, because once a dope boy, always a dope boy.

"I'm on my way!" Killa said, looking at the GPS's coordinates. It would take him a couple of days to safely transport that much coke. It was cool, though, because it gave Cam enough time to work out a deal.

****

"Hey!" Becky shouted when Cam walked into the leasing office. She knew, well, she hoped, he'd be back one day. Today was not that day.

"Sup," he blurted as he barged passed and entered Gloria's office and closed the door behind him.

"What's up?" she asked, taking to her feet at the intrusion. She wasn't sure what was going on and so prepared herself to fight if she had to. Her eyes shot to her purse where the little gun lived.

"You won't be needing that," he said, raising his hands in surrender. "I need to holla at Keith. I have a proposition for him."

"Keith? What you know about Keith? How you..." she asked and then answered with a look towards Becky. "I should beat her ass!"

"What makes you think she told your business?" he asked hoping to divert attention elsewhere.

"The same way I know your dick curves to the left, got a big squiggly vein running across the top, you grit your teeth when you cum, um... you..."

"I see," he cut her off since it was obvious that the white girl couldn't hold water. If she told all her own business, she'd definitely tell the next person's.

"Oh, and you dead wrong for just dumping her like that! Got her addicted to the dick and just cut her off!"

"Keith?" he asked again to change the subject. She was getting too happy talking about his sex life for his taste. "When can I meet him?"

"Come to the club Friday night and I'll introduce y'all."

Chapter 8

Michelle wasn't the type to nag or complain when she was upset but she wore her emotions on her sleeve so it wasn't hard to tell when something was eating at her. It began Thursday when Cam told her he was going out Friday night.

She trusted her husband with her whole, huge, loving heart, but couldn't shake the feeling his going out gave her. This was how her last marriage had ended. One day, Raymond Sr. said he was going out, that he had some business, same shit this one said. Next thing she knew, he was going out every weekend and several nights during the week.

He lost interest in sex around the same time women began calling his phone. He tried to compensate with the flood of extra money he was bringing in but all she really wanted was her husband back and for him to be a father to their boys again. The next thing she knew, St. Louis police were knocking at her door. He husband had been murdered in what was described as a drug deal gone bad.

"What?" Cam finally asked once they finished dinner. The rice was slightly undercooked and the meat a little overcooked, both which were unheard of in the Mercer home.

Michelle knew the most important and prestigious position on the planet was that of a wife and mother. For her to slack off in either area stood out like a sore thumb. Even last night's sex had been different. She'd mentally abandoned him as soon as he entered her. He was mentally preoccupied as well but still managed without her.

"Nothing, everything is just fine. I just don't want you going to a club with a bunch of young women, alcohol and drugs, but other than that, I'm just fine," she blurted. Again, she hated to be a nag but was proud to have spoken her mind.

"What would I want with a young woman when I have...um... That's not coming out right," he noticed. "Babe, It's just business. I'm meeting the owner to discuss business."

"Babe, you're a produce manager. What kind of business could you possibly have with a nightclub owner?" she asked, getting slapped with a sense of déjà vu. Raymond was doing business with a nightclub owner when he'd gotten killed.

"Either you trust me or you don't," he said, refusing to tell the truth or lie to her. "Now, is it possible for me to get a lil' bit before I go?"

"Of course!" she reeled. One thing she didn't do was turn him down for sex. He was a good husband and father which earned him unlimited coochie coupons. "I just came on this morning, but I got you!"

Cam happily followed her to their room. As much as he enjoyed their vigorous love life, he didn't mind when her cycle came on. That period of time is what men referred to as head week. It was kinda like shark week on animal planet except you got your dick sucked.

Michelle was relieved that he wanted sex before he went out. Raymond hadn't since he would get his while he was out. Instead of sitting at the edge of the bed, she went to the middle and removed her shirt and bra.

"Mmm," Cam hummed as he took one of her large dark nipples into his mouth. He removed his growing dick as he sucked on her titties before he made the journey north to her mouth.

"Stop!" she directed when his penis reached her chest. She answered the question on his face by placing his large erection between her breasts.

"That'll work," he agreed when she pressed her mammary glands around his shaft of meat.

He began a slow stroke between her breasts. Michelle met each upstroke with a kiss or lick on his throbbing head. The husband and wife locked eyes lovingly while he titty fucked her.

"Mmm, I'm gonna cum," he announced, giving her plenty of time for options. She leaned back and let him explode all over her chin and neck.

"Round two when you get back in," she dared as he spasmed and skeeted.

He almost said *fuck it* and stayed home, but once a dope boy, always a dope boy.

****

Cam had been perfectly content driving his regular sedan, it's what regular guys with regular jobs drove. That is, until he reached the club and saw the shiny, tricked out whips parked out front. St. Louis is a Donk town so there were plenty of older cars sitting high on huge rims and painted colors louder than the sound systems blaring from inside them.

"Y'all ain't got nothing on them BCB niggas!" he proudly proclaimed of his old crew. He'd been sixteen when he founded the Bubble Chevy Boys back in Decatur, Georgia. All he had to do was a buy a car and all of his followers followed.

He wasn't sure how long he'd been replaying old memories of when he was the man before he snapped back to the present. That was the past and here in the present, he was just a regular guy. A glance at his regular watch said it was time to head in.

"I'm supposed to be meeting Keith," Cam explained to the bouncer, hoping to avoid both the long line for regular folks and the high fee of the VIP entrance.

"Fo' what? Who is you?" the large man barked, proving that he'd been hired for his brawn not his brain.

"Let him in!" Gloria barked at him as if he were a child. She treated all of Keith's workers like that since there wasn't shit they could do about it.

"Thanks," he greeted happy to be saved.

"Mmhm," she replied curtly as she led the way inside. She could only hope he had some viable business because now was not a good time otherwise.

****

"So, what we gone do, boss?" Nate wanted to know. He knew that the Mexican Mafia were dangerous but would gladly go to war with them if given the world.

"Shit, it's our fuck up, so we gotta pay them folks," Keith sighed. HE was a million dollars in debt due to a two-dollar nigga smoking a five-dollar blunt. "They give Booger a bond yet?"

"Lawyer said Monday. Gone be high as hell and they gone keep tabs on him."

"Of course," the boss replied to both. Fifty keys was a lot of dope and the cops knew the moron was just a driver. They couldn't break him so they'd just watch him and see where he went when he got out. The first person he went to see would be the man. After all, he had some explaining to do.

"Who dat?" Nate asked, alternating his gaze between Gloria's cleavage and the man walking next to her.

"Some dude from Cali. Hope he got a plug. If not, plug his ass for wasting my time."

"Hey, babe, Nate," Gloria greeted as they arrived.

Cam noticed a flick of something between the bodyguard and her. He registered if for later and stuck out his hand. "Please to meet you," Cam greeted.

"Sup?" Keith greeted and slapped him five instead of shaking his hand. "What can I do for you?"

"Actually, it's what I might be able to do for you. My people got a few extra birds flying around. They need a home," he explained.

"I like birds; 'specially the pure breeds. What they going for?" Keith asked and leaned in.

Cam pondered for a second as if he hadn't already had a price in mind. At twenty-five grand, he and his cousin could walk away with over a mil each. "I can probably get 'em to go twenty-five on them. Got-ta do ten at a time, though," he bargained.

"Shit, we get them at seventeen now!" Keith shot back. That was what the Mexican demanded in return on consignment, but they'd fucked that up by losing the shipment.

"Okay, thanks for meeting with me," Cam said and prepared to stand. He could fuck himself for seventeen grand. Cam would sell that shit himself before he got chumped off.

"Hol' up, potna'!" Keith blurted with desperation audible to all present. "Tell you what, front me ten and I'll do the twenty-five."

"What's your turn around time?" he needed to know. That would tell a lot about the man's operation. If he said a month, he was small time and not worth the risk.

"'Bout a week, lil' less," Nate spoke up. They had traps all over town plus wholesale out in the suburbs. It wouldn't take long.

"I'll holla at my people and get back," Cam replied and stood.

"Call me direct," Keith said, handing him a card with his number on it. The music was too loud for anyone to hear Gloria suck her teeth at being cut out as the middle-man.

"Sho-nuff," he agreed and took the number. All eyes watched as he bee-lined from the club. They assumed he was in a rush to talk to his people but they were wrong. It was head week.

"You think he straight?" Nate asked, twisting his lips dubiously.

"Gotta be! Why else would he come?" Keith answered. "One thing I do know is, he ain't from no California!"

Chapter 9

"Ronald Bogeman, pack it up!" the guard announced over the PA system.

"Y'all set!" Booger cheered, using his last trump.

His fellow Spade players frowned at him in confusion. Dude was so used to his nickname that his real name hadn't registered. "Say, Booger, them folks just told you to pack it up," his partner said from across the steel, county jail table.

"Bruh, you got a bond on fifty bricks?" one of his opponents asked, cocking his head curiously. He wondered if dude was a liar or a snitch.

"Y'all niggas must fo'got who I fucks wit'!" he shot back. Actually, it would be impossible for anyone to forget since he had been name dropping since he entered the pod. It's actually a form of snitching known as dry snitching, which was another reason Keith was in such a big hurry to get him out of there. The hundred-grand cash bond had stung his pockets but he knew it would be coming back very soon.

Booger bragged and popped shit as he packed up his property. Had he really been the baller he was claiming to be, he would've given all the jail stuff away. Instead he packed his Ramel Noodles and honey buns and hit the door.

He knew it was his bad that the package had gotten knocked off, but in his mind, he still expected a coming home party. Most times when a homie came home from doing a bid there was a big shindig held in his honor with weed, liquor, music and, of course, vagina. Lots and lots of vagina. He had only been gone a week, though.

Booger stepped out the jail and spotted Snake in a sedan and rushed over. He'd barely gotten in good before he pulled the car from the curb. As expected, an unmarked car pulled out behind them. The cops focused on their target, therefore, they didn't notice two cars pull out behind them.

"Damn, cousin!" Booger griped at the quick departure as he fastened his seatbelt. He may drive around, music blasting, smoking weed, and speeding while transporting dope but he always used his seatbelt.

"My bad," Snake lied. He smiled in amusement at the seatbelt knowing it couldn't and wouldn't keep him safe. He only half-listened to the idiot ramble on beside him as he watched the police in the rearview mirror. The tail car tailing the convoy pulled off and bent a few corners. They would meet them in a few minutes since they already knew the route.

"I already know Keith throwing me a party! Prob'ly gonna try to surprise me, huh?"

"Yeah, I'm sure it'll be a surprise. A real blast," Snake replied. The ominous tone snapped Booger's head in his direction but he quickly distracted him by lighting a blunt.

"The hell is this nigger going?" one pink cop asked his pink partner. They both loved having a partner of the same race so that they could volley the n-word back and forth like a ball in a tennis match.

"Niggers," he replied, shaking his head. His head really shook when a car ran a red light and t-boned them. "Shit!"

Neither cop was hurt but they were out of the chase. The elder black man got out apologizing and getting cursed out and arrested.

"You see that shit!" Booger exclaimed at the accident that wasn't an accident at all.

It was his cue so Snake pulled to a stop at the next corner. "Huh? Yeah, wait here," he said and hopped out the car. Booger watched curiously as he walked briskly away. He was really curious when another car rolled past with Keith in the passenger's seat. They locked eyes until he was gone.

"See you on the other side, lil' bruh," Keith said and hit the switch. The plastic explosives under Booger's seat exploded with a loud roar. Booger was pureed like he'd been put in a food processor. "Let's shoot by the courthouse so I can get my bond back.

****

"I ain't mad at cha," Cam said when he put the events on the news in their proper order.

A drug suspect bonds out and gets blown up the same day. That had the Mexican Mafia written all over it, but he knew Keith had pulled the trigger or in this case, hit the switch. Either directly or indirectly. When he heard that he and Booger were brothers, he knew he'd done it himself. Cam was, or at least had been, a killer himself. Neither could add up to the killer who'd just stepped off the plane, though.

Killa got off the plane and scanned the surrounding area like killers do. A crooked smile contorted the corner of his mouth when he spotted his cousin. It grew into a full-fledged smile as he made his way over.

"What's good, cuz?" Cam greeted and embraced him.

"You, my dude," he said, squeezing him back. Killa and Cam let go and turned to leave the airport.

"What's up with that work?" Cam asked once they were rolling away in his car.

"Let's see..." Killa said, pulling up the GPS on his tablet. "They 'bout an hour out. You got a spot?"

"Yeah, I got a spot," he replied dryly. It wasn't a very good spot, but it was a spot. He lacked the network and resources to set up a good stash spot in Missouri. He'd thought about renting another apartment in Westwood but that would put both Gloria and Becky in his business. Gloria was too close to the action and Becky couldn't keep her mouth closed.

Stashing ten-thousand bricks in his basement was absolutely out of the question.

"This is your spot?" Killa reeled when Cam pulled up to a public storage spot.

"One of them. I got five around town. I'll just have to spread it around."

Killa listened as he laid out his plans to spoon-feed the coke to Keith ten bricks at a time. It was good money and had low risk.

"He won't try to fuck us over?" Killa asked after being told about Booger.

"Of course! But, I'll have his whole operation memorized by then. Once he passes away, I'll take over," Cam explained.

"Passes away," Killa chuckled. "You make it sound like he's elderly and about to die peacefully in his sleep."

"Won't be nothing peaceful when he die," he assured him. "Now, let's unload this truck so I can introduce you to my family and fire up the grill!"

****

"We need to find out who his connect is! If we cut these Mexicans out, we gone really get rich," Keith announced.

Nate paused to pick his words carefully. They were already rich and he couldn't understand greed. "Like you said, we fucked up. Let's just use this plug to pay the Mexicans back and get back to business as usual," he pleaded. Nate wasn't feeling the Mexican's demands of working off the debt and not making any money until it was paid off. Dealing with Cam could keep cash coming in and pay them off. A rare win-win situation in the win some, lose some world of drug dealing.

"Fuck them Mexicans!" he shot back, still high off his recent murder. Murder has the tendency to give a man a false sense of bravery.

Chapter 10

"What?" Cam asked, seeing Killa looking at him as he drove. It was obvious he had something on his mind so he invited him to get it off.

"I'm saying, though. I mean... Yo, you got a nice life, a nice family, you sure you wanna go back to that life?" he wanted to know.

Cam drove a few blocks in quiet contemplation as if searching for the answer. "Nah, you right. I do have a nice family. Good wife, good kids. I'm just gonna make enough to set us straight and then qui-," he said, stopping himself just short of telling a lie. As much as he wanted it to be true, he couldn't see it. Once a dope boy, always a dope boy.

"That's kinda wack," Killa said when they reached The Club. Keith had actually name his nightclub The Club.

"Actually, that's pretty dope! Err'body always saying they going to *the club*. Well, this is The Club!" Cam almost cheered.

"I guess," Killa admitted since his cousin was right. This club, like most clubs, was painted completely black on the outside. That made the bright lights that much brighter come nightfall. It was the middle of the day when they'd arranged to do the drug deal. "You sure you wanna front them the dope? Back when I used to hustle, that was a sure way to lose money."

"They'll be on point the first couple of times. I can count on them until they ask me for more. That's when they'll try me."

"And you know this?" his cousin asked, twisting his lips and brown.

"Know it? Shit, I'm counting on it. I got the work, so he'll take me under his wing. Show me his whole set up since he plans to kill me."

"Only, he'll die first!" Killa said because that's what he does.

The two men carried ten kilos into the club in two bags. Nate met them with a nod and led them up to the office. Cam scanned the area in a clinical fashion, as if he was trying to peep the operation. He wouldn't mind owning a club again, one day. Perhaps even this one.

"Welcome," Keith greeted with a smile as Cam and Killa entered the office. He eyes shot from Cam to Killa then from bag to bag before landing back on Cam.

"Sup, yo?" Cam replied once the man's gaze returned to his. They shook hands and he sat a bag on the desk. Killa came over and did the same. "This my cousin, Killa."

"Sup, Killa. What you do?" Keith asked, wondering what his purpose was.

"Kill people," he replied and took a position next to Nate as he inspected the coke.

There were fake smiles to accompany the forced small talk as Nate tested the purity of the product. He grimaced at the deep, rich blue the test strip turned on each brick tested.

"Boss, this shit is A-1! Pure cocaine!" he announced. The coke they'd gotten form the Mexican was good, but this was great.

"Where you get pure blow from?" Keith asked. He had to try them.

Cam pressed his lips together real tight to keep the sarcastic comments safely inside. Keith got the message and nodded in agreement.

"Call Quianna up here," he ordered and Nate complied.

A few minutes later, a sexy, light-skinned girl came in with a bottle of cognac and some glasses.

"Thank him, and him," Keith ordered as she poured the drinks. He pointed at Cam first so she handed him a glass and sank to her knees.

"Whoa! I'm good, yo'" he said, declining the blowjob being offered.

"I'm good, too. Gotta lovely little lunatic at home," Killa declined as well.

"A'ight then. Come by and hang out with me tonight," he insisted as his head waitress came around his desk. She dropped to her knees and began to unzip his pants.

"Will do," Cam agreed and departed before the blowjob got underway.

****

"Again!" Michelle moaned when Cam announced his plans for the evening. She could only pray that her blissful marriage wouldn't be over after just one year.

"You know my cousin is in town. I have to show him a good time," he reasoned with some kisses that smoothed her out.

It was still head week so she gave him a blowjob fit for a king. He watched his beautiful wife working her head, neck, lips, tongue and hand to please him. He was more than pleased with her and vowed to never let her go.

"You okay? You look woozy," Killa asked when Cam came to his hotel room to pick him up.

"Yeah, I'm good," he assured him, although he was still slightly lightheaded from the good head he'd received. "You ready?"

"I'm ready," he replied and followed him out.

The Club looked as different as night from day when seen at night compared to day. Being on the VIP list got the men in and up to the exclusive section in a flash. Cam spent the evening picking Keith's brain about the club while Killa watched the movement of the people. He made eye contact with a couple of guys one too many times and nodded to himself.

As expected, those same men stood to leave as Killa and Cam made their way out of the club. The valet took just long enough for the men to pull their car around before returning with Cam's sedan.

"I guess I could stand a new car?" he reasoned when the plain car arrived.

"That's how it starts," his cousin laughed. The money is just as addictive as the dope. Then comes all the nice things that it can buy. How are you supposed to stop after that?

"I think that car is following us," Cam said, bending an unnecessary corner to make sure.

"They been on us since we walked into the club. Keith's people hoping we lead them to a stash spot," Killa surmised. "Swing by the hotel."

Cam did and the men waited while Killa ran in and came out with a bag.

"This must be it!" Herb said happily. Finding the spot early meant he had time to get back to the club and get Quianna.

"Good! This means I got time to get back to the club and get Quianna! That bitch can eat a whole dick!" Jack cheered because good head is something to cheer about.

"Nigga, I got dibs on that mouth tonight!" Herb protested. The brief argument that followed was cut short when Cam pulled away. He put the car in gear and followed them once more.

"Where to?" Cam asked as they rode through St. Louis.

"I'll tell you when I see it," Killa said, scanning the area for the perfect place. A darkened alley beckoned so he pointed to it. "Pull in there."

"This must be it," Jack said as Herb followed them in. He had left just enough space between them that Killa was allowed time and room to hop out. He lay in wait as they crept forward.

"He stopped," Herb announced the obvious and came to a stop of his own. A soft tap on the window turned both their heads.

"Shhh," Killa shushed with a finger to his lips.

Herb lowered his window to hear the secret but didn't like it.

The silencer at the tip of the Tech-9 made it sound like someone spitting sunflower seeds instead of full metal jackets. Automatic gunfire made the men pop and lock until they dropped. Dropped dead, that is.

"You always get to have all the fun," Cam protested when Killa returned to the car.

"I'm Killa. It's what I do," he explained.

Chapter 11

"Nate, go on and drive Gloria home. I got business," Keith ordered without bothering to look in either's direction. Instead, he kept his eyes locked on some young girl dancing real nasty on the dance floor.

"Business?" Gloria huffed as she stood to leave. His cheating was one thing, but the disrespect was something else.

"Sure, boss," Nate said since he was the boss and all. He stood and led her from the club.

Keith waved the girl from the floor over before they'd even reached the front door.

"Hey," the woman barely out of her teens giggled at being in the VIP section with a real VIP.

"Hey yourself, lil' mama. Have a seat," he demanded as he raised a diamond laden hand to summon the waitress. "Champagne!"

Keith stuck his hand under the girl's dress and played roughly in her vagina. She squeezed her thighs tight against his hand but he forced them apart. It was a hint of what was to come.

****

"Where are you going?" Gloria barked as Nate drove past the street that led to her suburban home.

"The boss said to take you home, so I'm taking you home. To my home," he shot back and kept on driving.

"So what, I'm 'posed to suck your dick while you drive or something? Like some little young hoe?"

"That's not a bad idea," Nate nodded and leaned back to remove his dick from his slacks. He laid it on his lap as she crossed her arms defiantly.

She was just fronting, though, and soon reached over to touch it. She grabbed it, touched it and stroked it until it grew rock hard in her hand. She then gave it a few kisses before issuing a warning. "It's disrespectful to cum in the boss's wife mouth, you know."

"I know," he agreed as her hot mouth engulfed his throbbing erection. Nate turned the radio down so he could enjoy the sweet music her mouth made on his meat.

"Mmhm," she agreed and nodded her dick filled head when his body warned of its imminent explosion. She increased her grip but slowed down her stroke. Nate's legs rocked and he went stiff as he came in the boss's wife's mouth. "Just plain ol' disrespectful."

"Guess, I gotta let you cum in my mouth now. That'll make us even," he said, looking forward to sucking her dry.

"I'on know 'bout being even... But it'll be a good start, though," she said wickedly.

****

The young girl realized she had bitten off more than she could chew when Keith shoved more dick in her mouth than she could suck. All she could do was focus on breathing through her nose so that she could stay alive.

The man held her head in place as he savagely fucked her face, causing her to gag with each stroke. His grip got tighter and his stroke got harder as the end came near. The girl was a bit of a freak in her hood but this big dick was the big leagues. She'd sucked a few dicks but had never let guys cum in her mouth. It was obvious that she had no choice in the matter tonight.

"Drink that shit, bitch!" Keith shouted when cum escaped the corners of her mouth. He held her head with one hand while he jacked his dick with the other.

The poor girl almost had her tonsils knocked out the back of her throat from the force of his orgasm. Then she nearly drowned in the torrent of semen that shot down her throat. She let out a sigh of relief when his climax finally subsided.

"C-c-can you ta-ta-take me home now?" she whined.

"Home? Girl, we just getting started! Get out them clothes!"

She spent the rest of the night being repeatedly raped between snorts of cocaine.

The next day was business as usual between the two business partners.

****

"What's good, boss?" Nate asked as he sauntered into the boss's office at the club. "Heard you left with a PYT last night!"

"Yeah, and that pretty young thang had some pretty tight pussy. Had, cuz I beat it all to hell!" the man laughed.

He was right, too, because the young girl was at home with an ice pack between her legs, re-thinking the whole party/turn up lifestyle. It wasn't too late to become a CNA so she grabbed her phone.

"I ain't make out too bad myself," he replied but didn't go into details. She was, after all, the man's wife.

"You heard from those clowns you put on our out of town friends yet?" Keith asked. He had already heard from his traps and a few of his distributors that word on the street was that the coke was A-1.

"Nah," he replied, dialing Jack's phone. It went straight to voicemail so he tried Herb's and got the same results. The same result from both lines equaled one thing. "They dead."

"Probably," the boss agreed and turned to the news. Sure enough, their double homicide was the top story. "You think it was that Charles dude?"

"Maybe the Mexicans. They called about a payment," Keith replied unsurely. He was a killer himself so he'd recognized the murderous mirth in Killa's demeanor. Still, there was no reason for him to murder the men, besides the fact that they were late on a payment.

"Well, shoot them an installment. Tell ol' Charles we'll be ready in a few more days."

Chapter 12

"So, how's my daughter making out in college? Cam asked. Every time he asked their grandmother, she would say, "Chile please! That girl is a mess!" Whatever that meant.

"Um... About as expected. Straight A's, though," was all he would say. The dope girl was doing exactly what she'd been taught to do.

"Anyway, shawty hit this morning saying they ready to go again."

"Same thing?" Killa asked. He knew the moment they increased the buy would be when they were ready to try them.

"Yeah, if all goes well, I'll take it from here. I'll just send your bread wherever you want it."

"I'm good, cuz. If anything, shoot it to G-ma," Killa replied.

The cousins hit one of the storage units for another ten kilos of coke before heading over to the club to make the swap. Cam and Keith made small talk while Killa flipped through the cash and Nate tested the product.

"I want to open a club one day," Cam said. He almost slipped and added *again* but caught himself.

"This shit is a cash cow! Best way to launder dirty money!" Keith cheered and went into his whole operation.

"So, you think...you could like...learn me some business? I may open a spot back home," Cam asked sheepishly. Killa stifled a smile at his cousin's acting and continued with his count.

"Hell yeah! Shit, I may want to invest in you," Keith shot back. "I plan on retiring soon anyway!"

Nate looked up from his testing at those words. He planned on retiring the man earlier than he expected. The club, the operation and his woman would all be his. Killa and Cam caught it but Keith, in his arrogance, just kept on talking.

"I'll be through tonight, then," Cam said just as both Killa and Nate wrapped up their tasks. They both nodded that it was all good. Hands were shaken as the men departed.

"Did you see that?" Killa asked as Cam headed towards the airport.

"Yeah, I did!" Cam replied. His wheels were turning on how to divide and conquer. The fire was already lit. All he had to do was throw some gas on it and get rid of them both.

****

Cam didn't eat much pussy but when he did, he did it to death. Michelle writhed in pleasure as yet another orgasm crept through her body. Her spine tingled, causing her legs to shake violently. That signaled Cam to double up, licking and sucking her even harder.

"I'm cumming!" she shrieked loud enough to be heard over the PlayStation being played down in the den. The boys kept right on playing as if they didn't hear her. Their stepdad took great care of them and now he was taking care of their mom.

"Oh, I'm not done with you yet, Mrs. Mercer!" he warned with his face wet from her juices.

He lifted one of her legs towards the ceiling while turning her on her side. The froth from multiple orgasms allowed him to slide in 'til he tapped her cervix. Cam backed out and began a slow, steady stroke that rocked the bed.

Michelle knew nothing in life was free. This good dicking down had to come with strings attached. She wondered what they were, how long were they and if they would break. Another orgasm shook the thoughts from her head like an Etch-A-Sketch.

"Me, too!" Cam grunted in reply to her announcement. He pushed down to the bottom and skeeted on her womb's door.

"What you want, Mista?" she asked, sounding like a character from *The Color Purple*.

"Huh?" he asked, caught off guard. The plan was to dick her down real good then break the news in the afterglow but she beat him to it. "I quit my job at the market."

"You what?" she reeled. They were practically living from check to check as it was, so what would they do without his check?

"Chill," he said, reaching into his night table. He pulled out a couple grand and handed it to her. He didn't get the reaction he expected when she reeled away in fear.

"What's that?!" she demanded, hopping from the bed. Cam zoomed in on her bouncing breasts and missed the question. "I said, what is that?"

"Money. I been working at a club in St. Louis. I can make more money managing the bar than in produce! I..." he explained until she crumbled into a heap beside the bed. He rolled off and joined her. "What, baby?"

"My ex did the same thing. Went to work for some thug. He had him selling drugs then he killed him. Then that damn Keith Victor had the nerve to come to his funeral."

"Um..." Cam frowned as he pulled her into an embrace. He had already planned to murder the man; now he had another reason. "He'll get his one day. Trust me."

****

Cam enjoyed being back in the club. He eagerly learned the ins and outs of running the club. Things he'd known nothing about when he'd had one of his own. No wonder it had only lasted one night.

"You sure you don't want your dick sucked?" Quianna squinted in disbelief. The handsome man turned her down every time she offered her services. She was the head waitress not because she was in charge but because she gave everyone head. The only dick she hadn't sucked was his.

"I'm good," Cam said, holding up his ring finger to show off his wedding band.

"You know how many married men I fuck with?" she asked even though she couldn't quite put an exact number on them herself.

"Um...fifty?" he took a stab at it. It didn't matter since he would never be one of them. He may have been using a fake name but his love was real. Respect is a part of love so no way would he ever disrespect his wife.

"Um..." she said, twisting her pretty face in thought. The music from *Jeopardy!* played in her head as she counted dicks.

"Get back to me on that," he chuckled and walked away. Head week was days away by his calculations and then he would get all he could handle.

"We gon' be ready on that other thing," Nate announced when he caught up to Cam. In the month that had passed, they'd moved over a hundred kilos. They had just paid the Mexicans back in full. Now it was time to make his move. "We may need to double up. Maybe triple the next order."

"I'm just the man next to the man, so I'll have to ask," Cam lied. Seeing that they were ready to make their move let him know that it was time for him to make his as well. "Sucks being the second in command when you really do everything."

"Bruh! Who you telling! This clown Keith sit back like a king while I do all the work!"

"At least you fuckin' his wife," Cam laughed.

Nate hesitated to confirm what was supposed to be a secret then smiled and nodded. "Fucking the shit out of her!" he bragged. "He treats her like shit, too," he revealed.

"So, why be so loyal? Why set me up for him instead of just getting him out the way and dealing with me directly?" Cam asked. A terse silence followed, making Cam wish he had a gun on him. He did have his phone, which was just as dangerous. He hit the record function just in time for the man's reply.

"He is a dirty nigga. His dumb ass brother got us in deep shit with the Mexicans. He wanted to shit on them, too, until you came along. Now that he's paid them off, he plans to rob you."

"See, what sense does that make? Beat me for a few bricks when my people got it by the boatload!" Cam replied after turning the recorder off. He flipped it right back on to hear...

"We was planning to get him out the picture, anyway! Me and Gloria got plans for this city!"

Chapter 13

"Sho-nuff!" Keith said after the third playback of the traitorous recording. "Play it again!"

Cam managed to hide a smug smile as he played the recording one more time. It came with the warning that he couldn't do business with them anymore until he worked out his internal issues.

"Bad enough the nigga fuckin' yo' wife, but he wanna double cross you, too!" Cam instigated. He shook his head woefully as he added insult to injury.

"Bruh, I got ten-grand to take them both out!" Keith growled.

"That's not what I do. I'm a business. Handle your business and get back to me," Cam said and stood to depart. He saw tears of fury in the man's eyes as they shook hands. He went home to await the call. It would come sooner than he expected.

****

Looking like a scene straight out of *Scarface*, Keith snorted a line from the pile of cocaine on his desk. The little blue pill he'd taken would keep him rock hard while he awaited the return of his wife. She was out on one of her weekly shopping sprees that was one of the perks of being married to a kingpin.

"Bastard smoking in the house again," she muttered to herself as she smelled the stench of a cigar upon entering their home. "Honey, I'm home."

Keith took another line up each nostril, drained his cognac and then stood. His erection, ready for action, throbbed and quivered. He stomped into the bedroom where Gloria was stripping out of her shopping clothes.

"Huh?" she asked in reaction to him being naked and hard, something he rarely was around her. It was a question that she wouldn't like the answer to.

"Ugh!" he grunted and socked her with all his might.

It was plenty and she was sleep before she hit the floor. She awoke minutes later tied face down on the bed. She tried to open her mouth to speak but her jaw was too badly broken for that. Keith played the recording to answer her moans.

Gloria knew she was in trouble so she lifted her ass of the mattress and wiggled it. Her good pussy had gotten her in this mess now so hoped that it would get her out of it as well.

"Oh, now you wanna fuck your husband, huh?" he asked in a tone that hinted at the violence to come he stroked his Viagra-filled dick and climbed on her back.

Gloria willed her vagina to get wet and it did. He fondled her slippery lips like that was where he was going to enter, even though it wasn't. Instead, he spat on her anus and shoved his way inside.

She could only moan from the pain of both her throbbing jaw and him ripping her rectum to shreds. His dick was as numb as the rest of his body as he slammed in and out of her. His dick was coated with her blood and feces from the pounding.

"Nasty bitch!" he growled as he skeeted in her intestines. He was still hard from the Viagra and coke so he kept right on going. Minutes later, he shoved his dirty dick into her shattered mouth and came again.

"I'm sorry," she moaned sincerely. People are usually sorry when they get caught. She wasn't sure if he was finished or not so she wiggled her ass again.

"Save it for yo' boyfriend!" he said and grabbed her phone. He found Nate's number under the contact labeled *Daddy* and sent him a text. 'Come to the house.'

'Where's dickhead?' he texted back.

"Dickhead, huh! Made you rich and I'm a dickhead!" he growled as he texted a reply. 'He drove to his mama house. We got all night.'

'I'm on my way.' Nate texted back. He loved sticking it to his boss and there was nothing like fucking his wife in his bed. He pulled into the driveway and texted, 'I'm here.'

'It's open, come on up to the bedroom.'

Nate stepped inside and stripped at the front door. He gave his dick a few pumps until it was semi-erect so he could make an entrance. He took the steps two at a time and rushed into the bedroom.

"You ready for this dick?" he demanded as he stepped inside. He knew he was in trouble immediately when he saw her tied to the bed. Blood still oozed form her wrecked rectum. He spun to leave but Keith stepped from behind the door with his gun aimed at his face.

"Sup, potna?" he growled, fighting the urge to fire a bullet into his face.

"It's not what it looks like, boss!" he said, which was kind of crazy considering he was in his bedroom buck naked.

"Well, what is it then, nigga?" he wanted to know. He cocked his ear towards him for a reply but none came. "Thought so! Now, you came to fuck, so go on and fuck!"

"Huh?" Nate asked and got backhand-slapped with a nine-millimeter. Keith lifted the gun to whip him again but he gave in. "Okay! Okay!" Nate laid on her back and began to hump.

Gloria moaned from her broken jaw and wiggled but it didn't fool the man they had been making a fool of.

"Y'all must think I'm dumb! You ain't even in the bitch! Fuck it..." he said, cocking the gun.

"Wait! Hol' up," Nate pleaded. He spat on his dick and stroked it to erection. Gloria tilted her hips and pointed her fat mound of vagina at him. He slid easily inside and began to stroke it like it was his.

"Pussy good, ain't it?" Keith asked, hearing it squish.

Nate open his mouth to answer but a bullet to the back of his head shut him up. The next shot made the couple a couple in the hereafter.

Keith called his top men and told them to come to his house. He then placed a call to Cam and invited him over as well.

****

Cam, who was the last to be called, was also the last to arrive. This time he was armed and ready for battle. Although he knew that they needed him, seeing Nate's car put him on high alert.

"Up here!" Keith called out from the top of the stairs when Cam walked in. He had his gun in hand as he climbed the steps. "You won't be needing that."

Cam nodded but kept the gun out. He walked in the room and winced from the smell. It was an acrid mix of blood, shit, fear and spent gunpowder. The pile of death on the bed explained it as did the stunned look of the men around the room.

"Let's get down to business!" Keith order, calling attention away from Gloria and Nate. "Charles here is my new right-hand man. He does everything that piece of shit used to do. Except fuck my wife!" He went on to instruct them in the disposing of the bodies and then it was back to business as usual.

"Two down, one to go," Cam told the reflection in the rearview mirror as he pulled away from the house.

Chapter 14

Michelle put up a little fuss about Cam going out but it was just for show. She was happy to see her husband enjoying his new job instead of being the zombie he'd become while working at the supermarket. Not to mention, the extra money allowed her to quit waiting tables and focus on her family.

She knew her protest would land her in bed with him trying to make it up to her. It was worth it when they formed the perfect sixty-nine with their bodies. She deep throated his dick while he munched on her juicy vagina from beneath her.

The race to see who could make who cum first was on. She felt a tingle in her toes and clamped down harder on his dick in her mouth. She was almost done when he grunted and filled her mouth with his salty, slimy semen. A second later and she gave up her plum's juices.

She was still quivering when she mounted him backwards. Cam felt like a king as he watched her plump, black vagina play hide and seek with his meat. She rode them both to another orgasm before slumping off in a heap.

"Have fun at the club," she huffed as he wobbled into the bathroom to take a shower.

Cam didn't even look at his wife again once he emerged from the shower. He knew if he did, his dick would turn to stone and he wouldn't be going anywhere.

Michelle knew it, too, and found it amusing. She started to play with him and masturbate but knew it wouldn't be fair. Instead, she waited until he left and got one more nut before going to sleep.

****

Before hitting the club, he met up with Convict to show him the traps. He saved each distribution and trap house they stopped at into his GPS settings. He made sure to exchange names and numbers since he knew the future. It didn't take a crystal ball to know that Keith was the next to fall.

Convict seemed to sense what was in the works and embraced it. He knew he was just a sidekick and was cool with it. After all, when everyone plays their position, the whole team wins.

"Yeah, so, if anything ever happened to Keith, the show can still go on," he tossed out as they drove to the club. Cam turned and squinted at him, trying to figure him out. The man peeped it and explained, "I been out here for a few years but I'm from the A!"

"And, you know who I am?" Cam asked, wondering if he would kill or keep him.

"Hell yeah! You're the king! Cameron Forrest! I knew from the moment I saw you!"

"Who'd you tell?" he asked, getting a *come on, son* look in reply.

"No one. I'm with you, shawty!"

A month later, they had moved another hundred kilos. Cam sent half of the proceeds to his grandmother to hold and still had a couple of million in his stash.

Common sense urged him to quit while he was ahead, but once a dope boy, always a dope boy. If he sold the rest of the dope, his bloodline would be straight for generations to come, just like the Kennedys or the Rothschilds. Cam was thinking long term. It was really just an excuse because he loved the street life.

"Where are we going?" Michelle asked as they entered an upscale part of town. Her husband had been full of surprises lately. A shopping spree here, a gold watch there; always something.

"To visit some good people I know," was all she got out of him. That and a smirk that said there was more to it.

Michelle let out a long sigh as she stared at her man's profile. Cam felt her staring and lifted his chin to give her a better view. She felt her panties began to moisten as she looked over at him again. Another few seconds and they would've been wringing wet. A few turns later, he pulled into a gated home with a brand new minivan parked in its driveway.

"That's just like the one I want!" she exclaimed, pointing at the soccer mom express. It had all the bells and whistles to keep kids busy and the mom connected and comfortable.

"Oh," he said and got out. She hopped out of the same sedan he'd been driving for years and caught up with him. He rang the doorbell then opened the door and stepped inside.

"We can't just walk up in these people's house," she whispered in fear and excitement.

"They're expecting us," he shrugged as they walked through the large, empty living room and into a huge kitchen that made his wife gasp.

"Oh my!" she reeled, feeling more moisture seep into her lace panties. "I could throw down in here!"

"Mmhm," he said, moving on to the dining room before moving on to the family room and then the back deck.

"The boys would love that!" she said, pointing at the blue pool with a slide and basketball goal.

"I bet," Cam said and headed back inside and up the stairs.

Upstairs, they entered a stately master bedroom. It was also empty, except for one lone piece of furniture that was a dead giveaway to whose home they were in.

"Is...this...our place?!" she said once she saw the folding bed folded face down, ass up, just like the one at home.

"It is," he replied while unbuttoning his shirt.

She waited until he stepped out of his pants before pulling her dress off over her head. She then stepped out of her now soaked panties and assumed the position on the folded bed. Her wet box poked out from between her dark thighs and he couldn't help but give it a kiss. Next, he played in the puddle pooling between her swollen lips with the head of his erect dick.

"Stop playing!" she demanded and backed up on it. He slid easily inside the slippery slope and began to stroke. Michelle was so excited that she didn't last ten strokes. She came with a whimper and relaxed on the mattress.

"I see I'm on my own," he laughed and kept right on stroking. He didn't last much longer either. A few strokes later, he skeeted inside of her once more. Their new home was officially christened.

****

Another month and another hundred keys later and Cam was ready to make his move. The Mexicans were hot about being cut out and began to make threats. Cam saw his opportunity to strike and took it. He paid his way up the ladder and got a meeting with their leader.

"I have heard a lot about you," Cam greeted with a slight bow as a show of humility as he shook Padrino's hand.

"And I have heard nothing about you," Padrino replied. "In fact, it seems as if you did not exist until a couple of years ago. Did you drop out of the sky?"

"I guess you could say that," Cam said respectfully. "But, I am here now and I can help you with the problem you are having."

"The problem is respect! This...this...puto madre has disrespected us! First, he loses a package, then refuses to work it off. He pays it off with proceeds from cocaine from another supplier. I want to know where he is getting his cocaine from!"

"Me. I sold it to him at twenty-five grand apiece," Cam said and braced himself. His cards were now on the table so he had to tread lightly and see how things played out.

"You!" the boss shouted and jumped to his feet. His murderous henchmen all flinched, ready to kill on demand. He took a deep breath and regained his composure as he sat back down. "Where do you get your product from?"

"A friend in New York. However, the supply is gone and Keith will now come back to you," Cam lied. He had plenty of coke left, safely stored in Michelle's old house. He knew the danger of a turf war first-hand and wanted no parts of it.

"Keith cannot be trusted! If he betrayed me once, he'll betray me again!" Padrino stated.

He was right, too. The biggest mistake most people make in any type of relationship is giving too many chances. If a man cheats, it's because he's a cheater. If a woman steals, it's because she's a thief. If a person lies, it's because they're a liar. Giving them another chance is like equivalent to begging to be cheated on, stolen from, or lied to once more. They are all one in the same.

"Most definitely!" Cam instigated. "He has no honor. He will screw you over again."

Padrino frowned in thought for several minutes. Cam surmised that he was either slow or very calculating. He was a bit of both, as well as extremely dangerous.

"Kill him. I will give you his distribution network. Workers, stash houses...the whole operation," Cam offered.

"Why? What do you want in return? His cut? His percentage?" Padrino dared.

"Nothing. All I want is the club, free and clear, with no ties to the drugs," he said, symbolically washing his hands of everything else.

The boss went quiet again as he pondered things. He shot quick glances to a couple of men who were obviously his advisors. They all gave discreet head nods at the good idea. Padrino began to nod as well. He agreed to Cam's terms with one added stipulation.

"You kill Keith," he ordered in a tone that left no room for debate.

"My pleasure!"

Chapter 15

"Still nothing yet?" Keith asked when Cam came into his office at the club. They had run out of coke days ago and the effects were setting in.

Cam knew that a brief drought would help out everyone involved. It would make the dealers thirsty enough to work for Padrino when the time came. Not to mention that it would make Keith desperate enough to let his guard down. Once he did, he'd never get the chance to let it back up again. Not in this life, anyway.

"Nah," Cam sighed like it was true. He still had a truckload of coke stashed away. He had plenty of cash to live off, too, so he decided to save the rest for his comeback tour in Atlanta. The bits and pieces of news he'd received from his old city proved it was his for the taking.

"We gon' starve to death!" the greedy man lamented. He, too, was sitting on millions but that wasn't enough for him.

Cam was pleased to hear the desperation in his voice. "I know a guy in Mississippi that is supposed to have some work. He... Nah," Cam said and then waited.

"What? He what? Call him!" Keith pleaded.

"Can't call him. He paranoid as shit! I mean, I can take you to him, but it's gotta be just the two of us. You can't tell anyone, we gotta respect his operation."

"Yeah, yeah. Respect!" he shot back greedily. The man had no respect for anyone. Once he got hold of this new connect, he would squeeze him dry.

"Grab a hundred and let's ride," Cam said. Keith hit his wall safe and retrieve a hundred grand. The plan was almost perfect until they walked out of the club.

"Quianna, put that shit down and come on!" he ordered the waitress as she prepared her section for the night.

"Huh?" both she and Cam asked in unison.

Keith turned to him and explained. "This bitch is about to set the world record for the longest blowjob. She gon' suck dick from here to there and back!"

Cam started to protest until he saw the sadness in the girl's eyes. She didn't ask to become a sex slave. She just wasn't strong enough to say no to men. If a good man were to ask her to do good things, she would gladly do them. Instead, she'd gotten stuck around bad men who pushed her to do bad things.

Keith and Quianna settled into the backseat while Cam got behind the wheel. He set the GPS for Longs, Mississippi and pulled out. Keith pulled out some coke to snort and his dick to be sucked. Quianna let out a sigh and got to work.

"Steak, chicken...or both?" Michelle asked when she took her husband's call. The boys ear hustled from the side, hoping he said both.

"You decide. I'm gonna be a little late for dinner," he said, meaning a lot late. The roundtrip drive would get him home in time for breakfast, not dinner.

"Is everything okay? What's that noise?" she asked, hearing the slurps and sniffs coming from the backseat.

"I'm fine. Just a quick business trip," he said, not responding to the noise which would have been harder to explain.

"You need me to do anything?" she asked and meant it. She would literally do anything for the man who meant everything to her.

"Nah, I'm good," he replied after a moment of reflection. They both said their goodbyes and went back to their respective tasks.

"This lil' bitch sucks the whole dick, not just the head or the shaft, but the whole dick!" Keith cheered form the back seat. Quianna let out another sigh, this time through her nose since her mouth was full.

Cam drifted into his own thoughts as he sped south as fast as the law allowed. The couple in the backseat finished up and fell fast asleep. She still had him in her mouth like a pacifier. Cam had yet to come up with a plan, but still planned on returning alone.

****

"We're here," Cam announced as they pulled into Longs, Mississippi. Technically, he could have picked anywhere to go, but curiosity got the best of him. He had to come back to this sleepy town.

"What's that smell?" Keith asked, inhaling a wonderful aroma.

"Fat-Fat burgers. Quianna gone grab us a sack of 'em while we go handle our business," Cam replied. He pulled up to the shack and put the girl out to order.

"Hope this shit is worth the trip," Keith suggested as he came around to the front passenger's seat.

"I'm sure it will be," he replied. "I bet your team will be glad to get some work."

"Fuck them! I'ma sell this shit myself for a quick double up!" the greedy man cheered.

"Sho' you right," Cam agreed with his own decision to rid the planet of this scumbag. His GPS directed him to the small house his adopted daughter had once lived in.

"Someone stay here?" Keith asked and twisted his face up at the boarded up house.

"Yeah, round back," he replied and got out.

"I'm leaving the bread here until this shit check out!" he said and got out behind him.

Cam smiled as he led the man around to the back of the house. He discreetly pulled his gun out in front of him. They reached the back and Keith realized he'd been led straight into a trap.

"Motherfu—" he began as he began to pull his gun. He didn't live long enough to finish the statement because Cam spun around and fired a round directly into his forehead.

Keith's eyes went wide with the shocked look of the newly deceased. Perhaps he saw his place in the Hellfire because he didn't look pleased. He tipped over sideways and then dropped dead. Cam pumped a few more bullets into his torso for old time's sake and went back to his car.

"These...are...de...licious!" Quianna shouted between bits and swallows of her burger. Grease and Fat-Fat sauce ran down her arms and covered her mouth.

"I heard!" he replied and dug into one of his own. The burger practically exploded when he bit into it. He saw why Cameisha had gone crazy when she'd left hers behind.

Once they each finished their own, they split Keith's before ordering some to go.

Cam waited for her to ask about her former boss but she never did. He assumed, correctly, that she'd figured it out on her own. The only question now was if she could live with it or did she have to join him.

"If you could go anywhere you wanted to go, where would you go?" he asked, making sure to make it sound hypothetical.

"Atlanta!" she blurted instantly. "I had got accepted to college there, but didn't have the money to go."

"Now you do. Under one condition," Cam said.

"I know, I know. Suck your dick," she said almost sadly.

"No! Don't come back, and take care of yourself. Respect yourself. You're getting a new start in a new city. You don't have to be a fluff girl anymore!" He watched her eyes grow wide when she saw all the cash in the bag.

"You sure you don't want no head?" she asked gratefully. At the moment, it was all she had to offer. In a few years, she'd be a doctor and have much more.

"I'm good. I, oh..." he grunted at the sudden embrace.

She got out of the car and walked into the bus terminal without looking back. And why should she look back now that she had a future to look forward to?

Chapter 16

Cam enjoyed being a club owner just as much as he liked being a dope boy. He still had thousands of kilos stashed in their old house but that was reserved for a rainy day. At the moment, it was raining cash.

"This shit is booming!" Convict cheered as they looked out into the club from the office. Cam's new ideas doubled the nightly crowd.

"Sho-nuff," he replied pleased with himself. He was also pleased to have distanced himself from the drug trade.

The dealers out here were reckless cowboys. Many used as much coke as they sold and that was recipe for disaster. It was just a matter of time until one of them got caught and told on everyone else. Then they'd all fall like dominoes until they reached Padrino. No one could tell on Cam because he was legit. His timing couldn't have been better.

****

"What y'all tryna cop?" Jungle asked the two white men who pulled to the corner. He squinted and gave a grimace that made him look tough, but the truth of the matter was that he needed glasses really bad. Had he had some, he would've clearly seen that they were undercovers.

"What you got?" the passenger asked. He was unshaven with a scruffy appearance but further inspection would have revealed his clean fingernails and nice watch.

"Shit, dimes and dubs. But I can get ounces, too," Jungle bragged.

"Let us get a hundred worth," the driver bargained. It was the first of what would be many buys. Once the cops had purchased enough weight, they would make an arrest. He would be facing enough time to make him turn on his own mama.

"Who was that? Look like da police!" Cassie explained when Jungle re-joined the group of dealers.

"Nah, they straight. Took my number and err' thang!" he cheered.

****

"You up?" Cam whispered as he entered his bedroom in the wee hours of the morning.

"Huh?" she asked groggily. It was an act since she'd waited up for him every night. She had just taken a shower in case he wanted some when he came in.

He did. "Nothing," he replied, slipping face first under her short gown. There were no panties to prevent him from lapping at her luscious vagina.

"Ssss...Mmm...baby," Michelle moaned as he gently ate her out. He multi-tasked and came out of his own clothes at the same time. As soon as he licked her to orgasm, he slid up and rushed his erection inside of her.

It was too late at night and too early in the morning to make love so he fucked her. She pulled her thick, chocolate legs up to help him. Then she threw it back to help them both. Cam only lasted a few minutes before going stiff with an orgasm.

Life was good, but would it last?

****

A year had passed and The Club was still doing quite well. Cam was the perfect father and husband by day and club owner by night. Reports from Atlanta proved his children were all doing well. He decided to use the satellite phone to check on his grandmother and other daughter.

"Well, hey there!" Grandma Deidra sang when she took his call. "It's about time you called me!"

"I know, Grandma. I been... No excuse. How are you?"

It took over an hour and a half for her to answer the question. She had his full attention as she filled him in on her life. It was clear that she missed both him and his dad.

"So, how's the girl?" he snuck in when she took a breath.

"Who? The Dope Girl? Chile, please!" Deidra huffed and spilled the beans.

Cameisha had become quite the dope girl in the projects and then again at college. She'd tried to keep it on the low but the fact that she never asked for anything seemed to have said all that needed to be said.

"Xavier has been down there," she explained. If Killa was on the case, then the case was closed. Along with a bunch of caskets.

"Okay, love you, too," he said with a bright smile just as Michelle waked into their bedroom. A smile began to spread on her face until she saw that he was talking on "the phone".

"Love who?" she asked curiously when he hung up. She wasn't the least bit jealous because he never gave her reason to be. After a couple of years of marriage, he still sexed her like sex between them was brand new.

"My grandmother," he replied softly and waited for what he knew was to come.

"Oh," she said as if that were the end of it but he knew better. She fiddled in the dresser for a moment before turning and asking, "Why haven't we met your family? Are you ashamed of us?"

Michelle knew she didn't know much about her husband before they married. Some of his stories didn't match and others didn't make sense. He'd once even said he'd never visited California, yet that was where he was supposed to be from.

"I love you and my sons. My life... I... Trust me, I'll tell you everything one day," was all he had at the moment.

It was plenty and she left it at that.

Chapter 17

"Look at them two right there!" Cassie cheered and pointed to the two hoodrats on the dance floor. Both were putting on for attention and getting plenty of it, too. One was popping so hard that her titty popped out. It was deflated with stretch marks, but still a titty.

"Too pretty," Jungle said, turning his nose up at them He looked around the dark club in search of the ugliest girl in the place.

"What's up with you and pretty bitches?" Cassie wanted to know. The 6'1" Jungle was quite handsome but kept a two or three-star bitch by his side. "What you got against pretty bitches?"

"Too much work. Too many dudes and baby daddies to deal with. Plus, ugly bitches got the best pussy!" he exclaimed just as two aesthetically challenged girls walked by.

One had her short hair gelled down to her scalp. Dried red gel flaked on her pimpled forehead while the other had two different textures of weave attached to her hair. Both had tracks showing.

"For real, for real?" Cassie pondered while checking out the ugly girls. He recalled hooking up with a very pretty, highly sought after hoodrat a few nights back. Her vagina was so loose he had to keep checking to see if he was actually inside of her.

"Hey ladies! Come have a drink," Jungle offered, along with one of his winning smiles.

The girls checked them both out for a second before responding since they knew a drink came with strings attached. Strings that were attached to dicks.

"Hey y'all," Juanna sang in agreement. It was obvious that the men were getting a little money. If they were willing to spend a little, they could get a lil pussy.

Technically, it is possible to fuck in a club but a motel is a lot more comfortable. After a couple of drinks, the foursome headed to a nearby

motel for a foursome. Liquor was drunk, weed smoked, pussies pounded and condoms were filled.

"Damn! You was right!" Cassie cheered and high fived his partner
in between the twin beds.

"Told you!" Jungle nodded, having proven his point. It wasn't exactly true since most pussy is good.

"Right about what? Told you what?" Juanna wanted to know.

"Nothing," Jungle replied since the truth would have been insult-
ing. The box was good enough to want to hit again and he didn't want
to screw it up. "Give me your number, I'ma hit you up later."

"For real, for real?" she asked, since it would be a first. Most one
night stands ended after one night. She eagerly parted with her digits
and smiled the whole way home.

Jungle leaned back in his car, feeling relaxed from the good weed
and a good night. He was so calm that the lights from the police car
didn't even startle him. He put his blinker on and pulled to a stop.
"Y'all too late," he laughed to himself since he was absolutely clean. He
stuck both hands out the window so the cops wouldn't have a reason to
shoot him. Not that they needed one.

"License and registration, please?" the officer requested nicely. He
could afford to be nice since his partner had a gun pointed at Jungle's
head.

"Is there a problem?" he asked as he gingerly produced the documents.

"Is there?" the cop replied. He was just stalling until the narcotics
squad arrived. They confirmed the target and he was cuffed and carted
off to jail.

They let Jungle sit in a cold interrogation room for over an hour by
himself. It's the same principal as letting a stew simmer; it softens the
meat. He sat there wondering which of his many crimes had caught up
with him.

"Jack Rutledge," Good Cop announced as the bad cop followed him inside the room. Jungle vaguely recognized his government name since he rarely heard it. His mother gave him the moniker 'Jungle' when he was three because he kept climbing on shit.

"Nah, that's the King of the Jungle," Bad Cop quipped. "Ain't that right, you're the king?"

"If you say so. Why am I down here? Y'all ain't got shit off me, out my car, so..." he asked smugly.

"Oh, just a few hundred sale cases," Good Cop said, putting the picture of a familiar face on the table in front of him.

Jungle's eyes went wide seeing his best customer in uniform. "H-he-he a cop?"

"Yeah, and you sold him over a kilo of crack cocaine, kingpin status. Life in the Feds. Hope you don't got hemorrhoids," the other cop cracked.

"Kilo! King Pin! Man, I ain't never sold more than an ounce or two! Y'all got me fucked up!"

"Can you add? We can, and all those ounces or two add up to over a kilo. Welcome to the big leagues," Bad Cop countered.

"Or..." Good Cop stated and paused so the light at the end of the tunnel could flicker. "Or you can save yourself..."

"And your butthole. Unless you like getting trains ran on you. You might after those mud ducks you had in the motel last night."

The decision to fuck or be fucked is an easy one. Lucky for Jungle, snitching came easy as well and so the snitching began.

****

"Boss, you heard what happened last night?" Convict exclaimed as he rushed into the office at the club.

"No, what?" Cam asked, although he'd already heard the news reports of the early morning raids. Over fifty people ranging from street level dope boys all the way up to Padrino himself had been arrested. At least, that was the official version. He wanted to hear what the streets were saying.

"Bruh, err' body got knocked off! Niggas is already talking crazy, bruh," Convict said solemnly.

"About?" he asked, although he already knew. It had been over a year since he pulled out but fingers still pointed in his direction.

"That nigga, Jungle, is putting dirt on your name."

"That's because he's the snitch. Get Padrino's lawyer on the phone."

An hour later, Cam and Convict pulled into the gated home of Padrino. An armed guard escorted them inside where a balding Jewish man met them in the marble foyer.

"So glad that you called," the man said, shaking Cam's hand. The fact that he knew who he was, was not missed by Cameron. He'd obviously done his homework.

"Well, I heard what happened and wanted to see what I could do to help," he said in reply.

"We shall see. They are waiting for us in the study," the lawyer said, turning in that direction.

"Shit, dope," Convict whispered as he admired the plush digs of the drug kingpin.

Cam gave him that look a mother gives her child when they're out in public.

"Mr. Mercer," the lawyer introduced as they entered a roomful of Mexican Mafia lieutenants. Cam began to smile cordially, but it never fully materialized when he saw the stern faces all around. Even Mrs. Padrino had her pretty face twisted into a snarl.

"English! Me no speakie Spanish!" Cam ordered.

Convict snapped his head at him and gave Cam the same face he'd just given him in the hallway.

Cam knew full well that the sarcasm could get him killed but he'd rather it be here and now instead of putting his family at risk. Besides, guilty men copped pleas. He wasn't guilty so he held his nuts on them.

"This Jack Rutledge, AKA Jungle, is the only who received a bond. He left a club with some girl named Juanna, who said he got stopped right after he dropped her off," he laid out, proving that he had done his homework as well.

The lawyer began to nod his bald head in approval as the chatter in Spanish started once more. Mrs. Padrino stared at Cam as if she had x-ray vision.

"English!" Cam repeated.

"Why did you leave the business?" Padrino's wife demanded without a trace of an accent. "Surely there is more money to be made in drugs than in running a club."

"Surely," Cam agreed. Convict did, too, since his pay had been cut from the switch. "Less money but also less risk. I was sleeping safely while the cops were kicking down doors all over the city."

"True," Convict said, speaking out of turn. Although he brought in less cash, he slept like a baby at night. All eyes turned to him. "My bad."

"Do you think it is strange that you leave the business and everyone goes to jail? Everyone, except you?"

"That's because I didn't do anything to go to jail!" he shot back. "Look, I'm not your problem. I told you who was, now handle it."

"I must take my leave now," the lawyer said since the talk had turned to murder. Everyone was silent as he gathered his paperwork and left the room.

"We...I...would like you to handle it," the woman said, almost making it sound sexy. "Padrino would like you to handle this."

"It's not my business, but as a favor," Cam agreed.

All heads nodded in favor of the favor and the two men made their exit. They were both completely silent until Cam pulled away from the estate.

"Boss, if the Feds got them, then they got more than just the word of a snitch!" Convict announced.

He was right, too. Everyone Jungle gave up was put under surveillance so that a case could be built up against them individually. The Feds would work their way up from the bottom, turning defendants into witnesses until they got to the top. They knew full well that Jungle would be a dead man upon his release. Dead or in jail, it was the same to them.

"Plus, they gon' have eyes on him," Cam agreed. "Still he gotta go."

"Good thing I know where he gon' be," Convict laughed.

"Shawty, tell me you ain't gon' fuck Juanna man!" Cam laughed.

Convict shrugged and kept quiet since that's exactly what he planned on doing.

"I ain't mad at ya. I heard them ugly girls got that wet-wet!"

Chapter 18

"Damn, they were right!" Convict announced. He had to say it loud to be heard over the squishing of Juanna's vagina.

"Right...about...wh-wh-what?" she asked over shoulder as he pounded into her doggy style. She, too, had to speak loudly to be heard over the sound of skin slapping together and echoing throughout the motel room.

"Nothing!" he replied and kept on stroking.

He almost hated that Jungle was bonding out today. The Feds had let him sit for a few weeks before giving his family the money for his bond. Actually, they had paid twice. His grandmother had run off with the money the first time.

"I'm cumming!" Juanna screamed and did just that. She coated the condom with white cream that caused him to fuck her even harder. Convict was right behind her, literally and figuratively. A few strokes later, he grunted and filled the condom. Then the two collapsed on the nasty mattress to catch their breaths.

"Whew!" Juanna said, squeezing his deflating manhood. She squeezed so tight that it slipped out.

"Whew is right! You sure you got a man?" he asked again.

The pause that followed indicated her story was about to change.

"Well... I been kinda dealing with this guy. He locked up, but he 'posed to be getting out," she confessed. Jungle had been wooing her from the jail's phone since he'd gotten locked up.

"I see," he sighed and rolled out of the bed.

"Wait!" she said just like he knew she would. "We can still be friends! We can still hang out!"

"Yeah, I guess. You can keep the room," he said, tossing her the key. He flushed the condom before washing his dick in the sink.

"Call me tomorrow!" she called out after him as he left the room.

****

"What's wrong?" Michelle demanded when her husband simply rolled out of bed. She knew something was eating him when he turned down head week. She could always count on some professional pipe laying once her cycle ended, but today, he rolled right out of the bed instead.

"Huh?" he asked, having missed the question. The fact that he'd gone legit and still had to put in work was eating at him. If he did this hit, Padrino would own him. "I um..."

"You haven't spoken to me in days. You haven't eaten, and now you just hopped out of the bed..." she fussed.

Cam zoomed in on the sexual frustration in her voice. She was still carrying on as he slipped back in bed. That is, until he popped a titty into his mouth. That shut her right up.

"Mmm..." Michelle moaned as she grabbed his dick through his pajama pants. She squeezed and stroked it until it throbbed in her hand. She enjoyed head week just as much, well, almost as much as he did so she felt deprived. She snatched him free of the flannel and put him into her hot mouth. Now it was his turn to moan.

"Shit!" he cursed as he almost exploded instantly. He pulled out of her mouth and plunged himself in her freshly shaved box.

Now it was her turn to bust a quick nut. She shivered and shook while he kept on stroking. He got two more strokes in before he came himself. It was a testament to how turned on they both were.

"Better?" he panted out of breath.

She was, too, so she could only nod her head. "Mmm mm!" she protested when he attempted to get up. When she reached below his waist, he realized she wanted a round two. Round three followed that in the form of vigorous back shots in the shower. "Now, I'm better."

"Yeah, and now I just wanna take a nap," Cam laughed. He would have done just that to if he didn't have work to do.

"So, what's on the agenda for the day?" she asked in a tone that said it was a test.

"The boys have games today, so I'll probably take them for pizza after. Only if they win, though," he laughed at his joke, passing the test.

Michelle waited until her men left the house before calling Sheila. She'd made the mistake of venting to her when they'd run into each other. She complained about her husband being a little distant and the woman, who was husband-less, took it and ran with it.

"Chile, he got a chick on the side! Gotta have one!" she insisted. "He's handsome, got money, own a nice club, the most poppin' club in the city, at that! What you expect?!"

"Hey, girl!" Sheila sang, happy to have some company in her misery. "You, okay?"

"Yeah, I guess..." Michelle whispered noisily.

"Girl, what's wrong? He hit you? He looks like a woman beater! I knew..."

"No, no nothing like that. He made me cum so hard, I lost my voice," she teased.

The line went silent for a moment as it sunk in that she wasn't miserable. "Oh... um, yeah, that's good. I just thought he was up to something when I seen him at the old house," Sheila sulked.

"Oh, well, yeah, he goes there to check on it," Michelle played it off. Cam told her the house had been sold. He even let her buy a new car with some of the proceeds. Her curiosity was sparked but she wouldn't give Sheila the satisfaction. "Talk to you later, bye."

"Okay, I..." Sheila sang into the dead line. She let out a deep sigh and got dressed to go wait tables.

****

"Her lying ass," Michelle fussed as she pulled into the driveway at the old house. Nothing had changed since they moved away except the lock on the front door. It didn't respond to her old key so she went around to the side door but that had been changed, too. "Just silly."

Michelle was headed straight to IHOP to give her so-called friend a piece of her mind. She had just turned the corner when she saw her husband enter the block from the other side. She pulled over and watched him enter the house. Her heart stopped until she realized he was alone. A minute later, he came out with a small bag and got back into his car. He rushed back to the baseball field before the boys noticed he was gone.

****

"How was the game? Did guys win?" Michelle sang to her boys when they returned home. She may have been talking to them, but she was looking at him.

"Yes!" they both shouted excitedly. They proceeded to give her the details of both little league games at the same time.

"Is that right?! Oh!" she exclaimed animatedly even though she didn't understand most of what was said. Like quite a few women, she didn't know a touchdown from a field goal or a homerun. What she did know was that her husband hadn't been totally honest with her. He stood by smiling proudly as his stepsons gave the play-by-play details of their games. "Well, go get washed up and I'll fix dinner."

"They just ate a whole pizza each!" Cam exclaimed as if he hadn't eaten a whole one himself as well.

"Well, dessert then. How do cookies sound?" she asked. The cheers that followed proved it sounded great.

"I'm gonna lay down for a while. Gotta work tonight," he said, flashing a smile as invitation for round four.

"Okay, I'll put some cookies aside so the cookie monsters don't eat them all," she replied. She turned her back on that smile before it made her give in. "Oh, I gotta run to the store. Let me use your car?"

"My car?" he reeled at the unusual request. "Um, okay,"

Michelle rushed straight to the local home improvement center and copied all his keys. Come to find out, they both had work to do tonight.

Chapter 19

"Well?" Cam asked when he met up with Convict at the club.

"That snitch is out. Supposed to be hooking up with my girl later tonight. Prob'ly easiest to catch him in the motel."

"Mmm, your girl?" Cam asked.

"I didn't say *my girl*, I said his girl. The ugly chick, *Juwanna Mann*. 'Member that movie? Dude was in the WNBA?"

"Un huh," Cam nodded. He knew what he heard. Plus, he recalled bedding an ugly chick or two back in the day. He cold vouch that they had that good-good but so did most of the dimes he dealt with, including his wife.

Cam frowned at the memory of his wife asking a million questions as he got dressed for the evening. He wondered why she was so concerned about the old house but it made no sense so he shrugged it off.

"Well, I'm finna go keep an eye on ol' boy. I'll holla when they get in there."

"Aight," Cam replied and went inside. He spent a few minutes with the manager going over the details before retreating to his office. Once inside, he swapped his suit for black jeans and boots. Wearing all black, he was now dressed to kill.

****

"Boys, I'll be back in a few," Michelle announced and braced herself. She knew slipping out wouldn't be that easy with these two.

"Where you going?" the oldest demanded. He sometimes got their roles confused and though he was her dad instead of her son. It was only right since men are the maintainers and protectors of women. He was just practicing.

"Can I go?" the youngest asked and paused his video game.

"None of your business, and no," she replied individually to their separate questions. She got in her car and left her upscale neighborhood headed to their old one.

The drastic change in scenery hadn't been wasted on the smart lady. She wondered what she would do if she did find another woman. Would she give her lifestyle, depriving her kids of a father, and file for a divorce?

"Hell naw! I'ma beat a bitch up is what I'ma do!" she announced aloud as she mashed on the gas.

Michelle pulled into the driveway behind a plain sedan. She marched up to the door like she still owned the joint. The knob turned easily and she barged in prepared for battle.

"Huh?" she frowned curiously at a picture of her in a frame sitting on the cheap coffee table. Her husband had obviously taken it while she was sleeping. It had come out so well that she understood why he had framed it. But why would he have it at his mistress's home?

"Um... I don't know who stay here, but Charles is my husband!" she called out. No reply came so she explored the downstairs. There was nothing to see except for more Bargain Center furniture. The kind you could spend a couple of hundred dollars on and fill an entire room.

Michelle took a deep breath and let out a sigh at the bottom of the steps. She got her nerve up and marched up to where the bedrooms were. The two spare rooms were empty so she headed towards the master.

"I don't know who...hmp," she said, seeing that it was empty as well. If she hadn't seen Cam come in and leave back out, she would've given up; however, she did, so she didn't.

The only place left was the basement so she headed down there. She remembered having to do laundry in that musty dungeon before Cam upgraded her to their mini mansion. By the time she reached the bottom step, she was feeling really silly and really ungrateful for not trusting her husband. Then she saw the coke.

"What in the..." she wondered at the bricks of cocaine stacked neatly around the basement. She had seen plenty in the movies before but seeing it in real life took her breath away.

The hundred percent pure Columbian coke could be smelled through its wrappers. A large safe, standing an inch taller than her, beckoned her over. Again, she felt silly for trying the handle as if it would be open. It took a combination to give up what was inside.

A large collection of guns adorned a nearby table. She wracked her brain for an explanation for what her husband had going on like she always did when something was out of the norm for him. For instance, if he was late, she assumed there was extra traffic, but she was drawing a blank at explaining the guns and drugs.

On yet another whim, she entered her anniversary date into the safe and the lock unlocked. She held her breath as she pulled the heavy steel door towards her. A loud gasp echoed throughout the basement when she saw all the cash inside. Her knees buckled and she quickly braced herself to prevent herself from falling.

"This must be...a million dollars!" she exclaimed. She wasn't even close; it was millions of dollars. "Who did I marry?"

****

"He still in there?" Cam asked when he got in the passenger's seat of Convict's car.

"Hell yeah," he said, sounding salty. What he didn't tell him was that he'd stuck his ear to the door and heard that wet-wet Juanna possessed splashing all the way outside.

Instead, he passed Cam a copy of the room's keycard. Cam doubled checked his pistol for a third time and then got out. He looked both ways like a child crossing the street before he crossed the parking lot. He paused at the door and listened for a minute.

"Who pussy is this? Who...pussy...is..." Jungle demanded as he delivered firm back shots.

Cam took it as his cue and turned the knob.

"It's yo' pussy!" Juanna lied since it was not the time for the truth.

Cam's pistol sounded more like a cannon exploding when he fired inside the motel room. Jungle's head exploded, sending both blood and brain matter flying in the air like confetti as he slumped forward on Juanna's back.

"I ain't see nothing! I ain't see you!" Juanna pleaded. She ducked her head and raised her hands in surrender. Cam was a killer but he was not Killa so he spared her.

Convict waited until Cam pulled off before he pulled off himself. He would have gladly put the work in himself but respected him all the more for doing it himself. They pulled to the back of the club and entered through its back door.

"I only heard one shot," Convict commented hopefully. It would be such a shame to let good pussy go to waste.

"All it took was one. The girl had her head down," he replied to his relief, almost.

"What? You mean she was giving him some head?" he asked.

"Bruh, let me find out you strung out on that ugly chick," Cam laughed. Convict twisted his lips and Cam laughed louder.

Chapter 20

Cam awoke to a strange feeling so he didn't open his eyes. He could feel eyes on him so he lay there trying to make sense of it. He couldn't so he finally opened his eyes to investigate.

"What?' he asked of his wife staring down at him.

"Who are you?" she asked but didn't wait for a reply. "Sometimes, I call your name and you act like it's not your name. Sometimes you have a faraway gaze in your eyes like you are somewhere else."

"Babe, what are you talking about? I...oh," he began and ended when she placed a kilo on his chest. "You drove with that in your car?"

"Not funny!" she deflected his joke and stuck to the issue. "Who...are...you?"

"My name is Cameron Forrest and I'm from Atlanta, Georgia," he said with a sense of pride and relief. It bothered him to lie to the woman he loved every day. "I'm a dope boy. I was anyway, until I died."

"So, wha- I mean...who..." she struggled to ask a question. "So, how... Are we even married?"

"My name has nothing to do with anything!" he reeled at the implication. "You and the boys are my family..."

Michelle was in awe as she listened to his story. The real story came a lot easier than the tales he had been making up. He realized that he was losing her but still he kept going until he arrived at the day he met her at the restaurant.

"You have five more children?" she asked barely above a whisper. It made sense now as to why he was such a good father. "I can't. My boys lost their dad because of drugs. I can't put them through this again. I...can't go through that again. I have to get us away from you."

"I understand," Cam relented softly. He had just dropped several bombshells on her so he wasn't surprised. "Can I make love to you one last time?"

"I don't think that's a good idea," she replied, feeling her panties getting wet at the thought of his touch. She would have stayed strong had it not been for his touch.

"Okay, I love you," he said with a hug followed by a kiss and a fondle. Next thing she knew, her legs were on his shoulders and he was tapping on her cervix.

"Shit!" Michelle fussed as an orgasm came rushing at her. She came so hard that she shook an orgasm out of him as well.

"So..." Cam began once he caught his breath again. "Where will you guys go? Can I see the boys?"

"Go? I ain't going nowhere!" she insisted. He'd made love to her so well that it changed her mind. Everybody always talking about the power of the P. Now that's the power of the D!

****

"The streets is ours, boss! All we gotta do is move in where they left off!" Convict announced. The drought created by the large bust meant a gold mine for whoever came with coke and they had a ton.

"We gonna be in a cell with them dudes," Cam replied. He knew the Feds would be waiting for whoever came to pick up the pieces. Their conversation was interrupted by a breaking news story out of Atlanta, Georgia.

"Police in Atlanta are searching for accused cop killer, Cameisha Forrest. They say she is responsible for the death of an Atlanta officer along with another man in a mid-town parking garage. She is also wanted in Mississippi..."

"Who's that, boss?" Convict asked. He saw Cam turn white when the name was announced, so he knew she was someone to him.

"My daughter. I have to go to Atlanta!" he said and rushed from the office.

****

"Atlanta!" Michelle exclaimed. "I thought...I mean... Can you go back there?"

"No one's looking for Charles Mercer. Cameron Forrest is dead so no one's looking for him, either," he replied. The wheels began to turn just as he said it. Perhaps it was time to go home. Time for *The Return of the Dope Boy*.

"What?" she laughed at the faraway look in his eyes.

"Huh? Nothing," he said. Even if he could explain it she wouldn't be able to understand it. He saw the opportunity to become what he always dreamed of what every dope boy dreams of...being the king.

"Well, I'm coming, too!" she insisted and went for a travel bag. The way he had been laying pipe lately, she wasn't letting him out of her sight.

He opened his mouth to protest but she bent over to get her tote bag. "Hurry up and pack!" he decided when he saw all that ass. "We'll take the boys to your mom."

****

"We ready!" Convict announced when he took Cam's call. He was speeding towards the airport for their flight back to the city that had raised them.

"We?" Cam wondered into the line. He really shouldn't be taking his wife, so who was his partner bringing?

"Huh? Um..." Convict stammered.

"See you in a few," Cam shot back. He would get his answer once they got to the airport.

He got his answer when he saw Convict and Juanna rushing towards them through the terminal. He knew then that it was more than just good pussy. He liked that girl.

"Hey... Convict," Michelle greeted. She hated the dangerous nickname but knew he was close to her husband. She turned to Juanna and introduced herself, "Michelle."

"Juanna," she smiled and engaged in small talk so the men could make big talk.

"I got us a spot out in Cobb County and a car. Some heat, too, if we need it," Convict said, once again proving his worth.

"Hopefully, we won't," he replied. Hopefully, he could retrieve his daughter and get her out of there before she fucked up even more. He could only shake his head at what he'd created. She was a dope girl for real.

****

"Is he waiting for us?" Michelle asked, pointing to a driver holding a sign with his name on it. Cam bypassed the name on the sign and zoomed in on the man holding it.

"Fa sho!" he laughed, seeing his cousin dressed up as a limo driver. He raised his hand and played along. He even gave Killa a tip upon arrival at the house Convict had reserved for their stay.

"Thank you. Call me again when you..." Killa said, keeping in character until Convict led the women away. "No sign of the girl. Her phone is going straight to voicemail. Grandma is going to have our heads if anything happens to her!"

"I already know. I think I may know where she is," he surmised. He'd heard that she'd taken over his old apartment complex and knew it was a great place to lay low.

"Well, get straight and I'll swing back in a couple of hours," he replied and departed.

Cam intended on getting a little action before they headed out. It was impossible to get laid on the plane in the new age of scrutiny and security. He obviously wasn't the only one with romance on his mind. The sound of sex could be heard as soon as he walked in.

"Dang, Convict. Already?" he mused when he heard the mattress and headboard singing back up to the skin slapping and moans.

"As soon as they walked in!" Michelle laughed even though she had the same thing on her mind as well. She led her husband down the hall and into the room they would be using during their stay. "Strip!"

"Just gonna take the dick, huh?" he mumbled as he complied. The couple had been married for years but every time he watched her strip, it was like the first time all over again. He had a raging erection by the time she stepped out of her lacy panties.

The couple engaged in a make-out session while she stroked his dick. It didn't take long before he released his excess excitement. That ensured that he would last a long time inside of her.

Michelle mounted her husband and smothered his mouth and face in wet kisses. She rode him to an intense orgasm and fell off to the side. Cam contemplated which position to put her in before deciding on her favorite

He lay his wife flat on her stomach and arched her ass towards him. Her vagina practically sucked him inside. She wiggled and rocked while he grinded and stroked. Minutes later, he filled her full of semen.

"I gotta go," he said reluctantly. As much as he would have liked to stay there inside of her, he had to go find his daughter before she did any more damage.

Chapter 21

"Man, it feels good to be back in this city!" Convict admitted as they drove through the heart of Atlanta.

Cam felt the same way but didn't want to admit it. "Yeah, it do," he confessed. It was at that moment he knew for sure that he was coming home.

The ride out to Decatur isn't very long but it was very quiet as each man dealt with the demons that drove them from their beloved city. Both realized the coast was clear to return. And with the amount of coke they had, the city would be theirs for the taking.

"Right there," Convict said, pointing at an apartment when they pulled into Eastwyck.

Killa confirmed it was him when he stepped out on the small concrete steps, then went back inside. Cam led the way and entered the apartment. It was set up like a typical man cave with a leather sofa and a big ass T.V. A blunt smoldered in the ashtray like incense.

"Don't mind if I do," Convict announced and hit the blunt.

Killa and Cam both declined when he tried to pass it.

"No sign of the girl," Killa sighed. Not only did he not want to deal with grandma but he was quite fond of his niece.

"Let's ride over and holla at Bigs. Maybe he seen her," Cam suggested. It was a long shot but better than no shot.

"I'll swing through the trap and see what's what," Convict offered.

Cam nodded at the good idea and left with his cousin.

****

"Who?" Big Shawn shouted from his sofa. He had an idea of who it was since no one just popped up at his spot except one person. The chick in his lap attempted to lift her head from the head she was giving but he held her in place. "I said who!"

"Killa and Cam," Killa chuckled as he let himself in followed by Cam. Big Shawn deflated instantly inside his guest's mouth.

"G-g-g-go on in my room. I'll be th-th-there in a sec," he told the woman. She complied with all eyes on her ass as she left.

"Kinda young ain't she?" Cam asked of the college aged female. She was legal but Bigs was fifty-something at this point.

"Fuck I wanna fuck with women my age for?" he wondered. No one could answer despite the silence that followed.

"Anyway, you seen my daughter?" Cam cut straight to the chase.

Shawn went flush, which answered before he even opened his mouth. "She was here last night. She came for... Sampson," he replied, spinning the room into silence once more.

"Why in the world would she want that?" Killa asked out loud. A silly question really since a suicide vest only serves one purpose. "Why would you sell her that?"

"Her boyfriend got shot in the head last night. She killed a cop and that scumbag from home, Suave. She was dating his brother at one point and he's dead, too."

"But why sell her a suicide vest?" Cam asked in a whisper just below a growl. The pain of losing his father to the device flooded his memory banks until they overflowed.

"Sell! She stole it! At gunpoint! Threatened to shoot me!" he blurted, hoping to calm the man.

"That sounds like Cameisha," Killa said. "Now, who she planning on taking with her?"

****

"An explosion rocked a funeral today. Early reports put the death toll at fifteen with more than thirty injured including ten in critical condition at area hospitals. Police say wanted fugitive, Cameisha Forrest, is to blame. She was last seen approaching the mourners and detonating herself..."

"How is that funny?" Michelle reeled as her husband rolled in laughter beside her.

He was laughing so hard that tears streamed down his face. It took several minutes for him to regain his composure. "You wouldn't understand. Anyway, get dressed. We're going to church," he replied as he rolled out of bed.

"Oh, okay," she pouted slightly. Actually, she wanted to make love but church was good, too. A shower rinsed away the residue of last night's sex before she selected a dress to wear.

Cam was fully dressed and dapper when she emerged from the bathroom. Both Convict and Juanna were dressed and ready when they came out of their room. They were shocked that Juanna actually looked cute in her church clothes.

"Juanna?" Cam asked and squinted to make sure it was really her.

"I know, right!" Convict laughed.

"Y'all so silly!" Juanna said, missing the joke once more.

"Yeah, they are, girl," Michelle agreed before taking her by the crook of her arm. "Come on, let's go."

No one asked but everyone wondered why, with all the mega churches in Atlanta, Cam picked a modest one on the city's Westside. The preacher was preaching a good one when they walked in but that wasn't why they were there. In fact, it was obvious to his observant wife that he wasn't even listening. She followed his eyes to an elderly woman sitting with a couple of young teens. The girl was pretty and obviously bored. It wasn't until the boy turned his head to the side that she figured out who they were.

"Your children?" Michelle asked happily and squeezed his hand.

"Yeah," he nodded proudly, never taking his eyes off of them. He watched them until the pastor announced for the sixth time that he was done preaching for the day. "Let's go."

"Wa-wait, aren't you going to speak to them?" Michelle whined as she rushed to keep up with her husband. She was ready to have them join the family. She always wanted a daughter and had been mentally doing the girl's hair during the service.

"Not right now," he replied. Once again, he sat back and watched his family as their grandmother drove them away. He knew where they were going so it was no need to follow. He would make his way to the house in a day or two. In the meanwhile, he had a funeral to attend.

Chapter 22

Cam watched in utter amazement as Cameisha's rag tag little team assembled at her so-called gravesite. He could place a name to every face just by what he'd heard about them. The white girl was the scientist named Samantha. The jet black beauty crying her eyes out was Jackie and the big girl with the baby had to be Aqua.

He had no idea who was in the box but he knew damn sure that it wasn't Cameisha. The smirk on Aqua's face proved it. It also proved that she was the closet person to his daughter. He waited until the casket was lowered and everyone had left before making his approach.

"Well done, lil' mama," he said, clapping as he walked. He was very impressed by her move.

She had learned from the best, his father.

****

Cam headed east to Decatur to see his other kids by Shay and Britney. He pondered the whole way there whether or not he should let Britney in on the fact that he was back. She was older but hadn't matured more than a few days in the years that he'd been gone. According to her social media, she still liked to turn up, get drunk and get high.

"Nah," he'd decided by the time he reached their subdivision.

Ms. Thompson had just pulled up in a mini-van when he reached the end of the cul-de-sac. He watched in amusement as six kids piled out as if it was a clown car. He recognized his three by the two sisters. The other three were also Britney's by three other men. Turn up, indeed.

His oldest, Shanay, obviously felt his presence because she turned her head in his direction. She squinted, frowned, smiled, then took off running in his direction.

"Daddy!" she screamed as she ran towards the car.

Cam stepped out just as she leapt in the air. "Hey, baby girl!" he smiled, catching her and hugging her tightly. The other kids caught on and ran towards him as well. Even the ones he hadn't fathered yelled 'Daddy' and hugged him tightly. They'd never met their fathers and didn't know any better.

"Cam, is that you?" Ms. Thompson asked. She blinked rapidly to make sure it was really him. The closer he came, the more she blinked. "It is you!"

"Yes, it's me. Is Britney here?" he asked cautiously, looking towards the house. Again, her social media accounts revealed that she told all her business. He certainly didn't want her telling his.

"Chile, ain't no telling where that girl is. I would call her but she gone think her kids need something and reject it," she huffed.

He could tell that she was frustrated by her daughter's antics, but it was perfect for him. He spent a couple of hours playing with his children and their siblings.

"Ms. Thompson, I'm finna go," he said and smiled. He hadn't used the word *finna* in years and couldn't help but grin when he heard it come out of his mouth.

"Come on up for a minute before you go!" she called from upstairs.

He excused himself and headed up to see what she wanted. "Yes ma'am...you trippin'," Cam laughed when he saw her laid out on the bed. He felt his dick jump at the memory of how good the sex had been. Pussy gets better with age so it was probably even better than before.

"Take care of me real quick...sss...before you go," she pleaded, playing in her pussy. It got wet and glistened on her fingers right before his eyes.

"No can do. I'm married," he said, holding up his wedding band clad finger as proof.

"If I had a dollar for every wedding band some married man put in this pussy...I'd be rich," she said, running her finger over her juice box.

Curiosity got the best of him so he watched as she literally fucked herself. She was so excited by having an audience that she came in minutes.

"You straight?" he chuckled while she shivered from the orgasm.

"I guess. Get on out of here and close my door," she said and went for round two.

****

Cam's next stop was on the southwest side of Atlanta. He had purchased a house for Trish's mom years ago when she first took his kids. He was pleased to see how well-maintained it was as he approached. When he got closer, he saw something that pissed him off.

"Yeah, lil' mama, come on go for a ride," a twenty-something-year-old man was saying from a car as he fondled a girl's ass.

"I cain't! My grandma be trippin'," she pouted. She was only half telling the truth. Her grandmother did run a tight ship but she was also far from fast. She liked to dress fast and act fast but she wasn't fucking.

"KAYLA!!!" Cam demanded as he pulled to a screeching stop in front of the man's car. He wisely threw it in reverse and got up out of there.

Kayla frowned as if she was seeing a ghost. Once if fully registered that it was her father, she sucked her teeth and stormed off into the house.

"I bet," Cam laughed to himself and followed her. He knocked on the storm door as he let himself in. "Kayla, Cameron!"

Sixteen-year-old Cameron Forrest the Third stormed into the room to investigate the man's voice in their home. He wore an appropriate scowl at the intrusion. His reaction was the complete opposite of his sister's. A huge grin threatened to split his face in two when he saw his father. "Sup, Dad?" he grinned and greeted him with a pound and a man hug like he did with his peers.

"You," Cam replied staring at his twin. "Sup with your sister?"

"Her graduation was last week," he explained, which explained it all. The daddy's girl had endured life without her daddy by promising herself that he would be at her graduation.

"I see," he agreed. "I'll make it up to her. I'll make it up to you both. What's her favorite color?"

"Pink! The girl got pink purses, pink shoes pink..."

The next morning, she had a pink SUV sitting in the driveway. On it was a big pink bow and a little pink card with her father's phone number.

Father and daughter made up over a two-hour phone call that ended with a promise.

"I'm coming home and I'm never leaving again."

****

"This place is perfect! Better than the spot back home! I mean in St. Lou, cuz this is home!" Convict corrected. Now that it was settled and they would be coming home, it was time to setup shop.

"We shall see," he sighed as they pulled into the parking lot of Club Illusions. The parking lot was already a step up from the club he owned in back in his adopted city.

Convict pulled the rented Benz up to the VIP section and got out. He traded the keys to the valet for a ticket then stepped to the bouncer.

"Tell Breeze Mr. Mercer has arrived," he ordered quite professionally.

The bouncer was use to taking orders so quickly relayed the message. "Someone will be right out," he said, removing the velvet rope to grant them partial entrance.

A couple of minutes passed before a pretty mulatto woman with short hair came out to greet them. "Mr. Mercer?" she asked, flashing a smile while extending her hand in between the two men so that whichever one was him could take it. "I'm Billie."

"Please to meet you," Cam said, taking her outstretched hand.

"Follow me," she announced and spun on her heels. The modestly dressed woman could not conceal all the ass she was toting. It jiggled and jumped under her skirt as she led the way to the office where the boss awaited. "Brezel, Mr. Mercer."

"Nice to meet you," Breeze said as he stood. As he extended a hand to his guests, he and Billie shared a quick glance that showed they were together.

"Likewise," Cam said cordially. He loved the role of sophisticated businessman far more than street thug.

"I'll leave you guys to talk business," she said and excused herself. This time only Breeze watched her ass on display as she left.

"So, why you wanna sell this club?" Convict had to ask. He spoke out of turn but since it was in the air, Cam sat back and waited for an explanation.

"I don't want to sell it. I have to. My ex-manager screwed up my books so bad that it's the only way I can stay out of jail," he admitted. The heavy sigh that accompanied the confession proved its veracity.

"The price a bit high," Cam lied, looking for room to negotiate.

"Yeah, right," Breeze chuckled knowingly. "Tell you what. You guys head on up the VIP on me. Have your people call my people Monday and see what we can come up with."

The two legends of the underworld stood and shook hands like the gentlemen they had evolved into. Normally, on a personal level, Cam didn't like the club scene. For him, it was always strictly business but tonight, he decided to let his hair down and enjoy himself.

"This is bigger than our spot," Convict said as the entered the VIP section. He had a penchant for pointing out the obvious that amused Cam. Cam also noticed his use of the word *our* when talking about *their* business. It proved that he was not only a team player, but also on Cam's team.

"Yeah," he agreed and scanned the celebrity faces in attendance. Each had thousands of dollars' worth of champagne and liquor at their respective tables. Someone obviously had slipped a little weed in their hookah, giving a slight fruity aroma to the tobacco.

Cam looked out on the dance floor at the party people enjoying themselves. The sophisticated patrons swayed and clapped to the R&B being spun by the DJ.

"Look at your auntie!" Convict laughed, pointing at an older lady twerking on the dance floor.

"Leave my..." Cam began but was cut off by the sight of two young girls on the dance floor. One was twerking so hard that her little dress rose up over her hips, putting her ass on full display. The little hoochie mama next to her kept tugging on her little dress to prevent it from doing the same. Cam raised a hand to summon a waitress. "A bottle of Dom and send those two up here."

"Those two?" the waitress asked with a confused frown. He certainly didn't look like the type to be interested in those types.

"Those two," he repeated.

She shrugged her opinion and set off to collect his order of expensive champagne and cheap girls.

He watched the girls clap and bounce when she delivered the invitation. The looser of the two led the march up to VIP. The look on her face said she had made it.

"Boss, I'm good on the young girls. Juanna take care of me so well, I don't even fuck around," Convict said. He almost second guessed his mentor until the girls arrived.

"Y'all wanted some company?" the first one demanded a hand on her little hip. The second one was a little shy and kept her eyes low until Cam spoke.

"Sure," he said, causing her to look up and choke.

"Daddy!" she shrieked, cold busted. She'd left the house headed to the movies wearing a tasteful outfit. However, her hoochie friend, Bianca, had talked her into going out. She let her use one of her fake IDs to gain entry into Atlanta's hottest club.

"YES, DADDY!!!" he boomed and stood.

Convict stood, too, knowing the night was over. Cam snatched his daughter by the hand and began to march away. Convict followed while Bianca was stood frozen in place. She called a lot of older men daddy, so she couldn't figure out what was going on.

"You, too!"

"Oh," she jumped and followed as well.

"Now, I'm definitely buying the club, to keep the two of you out!" he snapped as he drove.

Chapter 23

"I'm going to miss this place. This city, my church," Michelle went on as the moving men loaded their belongings on the forty-foot truck that would move them to their new home in their new city.

Cam let her pick out a swank, gated estate in the Vining area of town. She loved the house but Tyler Perry living a few houses down sealed the deal. The new house came with a new Cadillac truck since she didn't want to drive her old one across country.

"I guess you can stay here. Me and the boys..."

"Yeah, right! The boys can go or stay but you ain't going nowhere without me!" she clarified. She knew her sons would one day leave the nest but he was her mate for life.

"So, get out the men's way and let them pack!" he said, pulling her into his arms. They shared a peck that transformed into a passionate kiss. Normally, they would've ended up in bed but it was packed on the truck already.

"Mmm, I wish you were flying with us. I'd figure out a way to get you in that bathroom and..."

"We ready, Mom!" Brian announced as he and Raymond burst into the room.

"Hold that thought," he said with one final kiss.

The taxi to the airport arrived a few minutes later and he saw them off. As soon as they pulled away, he called Convict.

"Just dropping her off at the airport. I'll meet you at the house," he said upon taking the call.

That was all that needed saying so they both pressed the end button and terminated the call.

****

The full weight of the mission hit Cam when he pulled up to the stash spot. Moving that much coke across that many state lines would put them both under the jail. Actually, the Feds had a prison underground for shit like this. The look on Convict's face when he arrived said that he was feeling the same way.

"Sup, shawty?" he greeted with a lump in his throat.

"Listen up, bruh. We gon' be aight," Cam announced. "Now, let's get this shit boxed up fo' the movers get here."

"Movers?" Convict asked with delight. He'd assumed they were driving the dope to Atlanta.

"Hell yeah! Wait... You didn't think... Boy, stop!" he laughed.

For the next several hours, the men loaded coke and cash into moving boxes. They placed plates and other knick-knacks on top just in case someone opened them. No sooner had they finished than the truck pulled up.

Cam felt a twinge of something as he watched the men load thousands of pounds of cocaine. Poor fellows hand no idea of what they were hauling. When the truck was loaded, Cam and Convict got into a rental to follow them to Atlanta.

"We're going home, shawty!" Convict cheered. The words finally hit all the way home.

"Yeah, we going home."

****

By the time the sale of the club went through, it had been shut down. That actually worked in his favor, giving him a blank canvas to create from. He now knew enough about the business to act as his own manager.

An ad in the paper made droves of people to apply for the various positions that needed to be filled. He couldn't help but be amused at having to interview police officers to work security. A fresh faced young officer caught his attention. He was big and burly enough for the position but something about him was also familiar.

"Where you from?" Cam asked curiously.

"Eastside, Decatur but I live nearby so..." he explained.

"Who are your parents?" Cam demanded, startling the young man.

"My mama name is Damita and my daddy was Ant. He got killed when I was little," he confirmed.

"Don't know 'em," Cam lied. In truth, he'd fucked his mom back in the day and had his father killed. "You got the job."

Anthony smiled just like his father had when they were friends a lifetime ago. He felt no remorse for the murder since it came with the game they'd chosen to play. Ant had tried to cross him and got crossed out instead.

"Thanks, Mr. Mercer!" he said and shook his hand.

Cam was just as happy to have a cop working for him.

"Look who I found!" Convict cheered as he escorted Quianna up to the empty VIP. She had no idea who owned the club when she'd answered the ad for a waitress. Cam wasn't sure how to take her presence until she spoke up.

"I'm in school now," she proclaimed proudly. "And I sing at my church!" She could have gone on and on naming all that she'd accomplished since they'd last seen each other. All it had taken was a little self-esteem to jump start her life. Once a good girl has gone bad, she may be gone for good, but the opposite applies for bad girls gone good.

"That's wonderful," Cam said with a light applause. "I want you to supervise all the waitresses. Don't let me down."

"Thank you. I won't!" she promised and ran over to hug his neck. "I owe it all to you!"

"Next!" Convict called out, bringing the next familiar face in.

"NO!!!" Cam shouted immediately.

"But I need a job, Daddy!" Kayla protested.

"Girl, you too young to be waiting tables!" he shot back.

"Wait tables? Boy, stop!" she huffed with her hand on her hip. Only for a second until his eyes went wide at the gesture. "Daddy, I'm finna major in accounting. I want an office job."

"Okay. You can be the assistant to the accountant. He works during the day," he agreed with a smile. Kayla twisted her lips in defeat.

"Okay," she pouted, having gotten half of what she wanted.

"So, when we gon' really set up shop?" Convict asked once the positions had all been filled.

He had been conducting interviews himself all over town. A team was on standby ready to move on command. The demise of the Salazar family had left a void in the city's drug trade. Prices were sky high and they could make a killing.

"Too soon, bruh," Cam advised. More dope boys on the street meant police would have to spread their resources thin to watch them all. If he moved now, it would be all eyes on him.

"You right!" Convict agreed once he explained it to him.

Chapter 24

The wait lasted almost a year. During that time, several players had moved in and gotten knocked off. Convict's plan to spread the work all over the city was on point. This way, the police had no idea where it was coming from.

"Say what?" Convict reeled when he heard Cam's plan. "We giving the shit away!"

"Not really. Three-hundred an ounce leaves plenty room for everyone to eat," he explained. It was true, but in actuality, he really just wanted to get rid of the stuff. At ten-grand a key, he would still make millions.

"You the boss," Convict sighed. He hit the stash house then began the task of supplying the traps. It was all good until he reached Decatur, which was Cray-Cray's turf.

Cray-Cray was an absolute wild man but he moved a lot of work. His motto was ball until you fall; until he fell. He fell out with Cameisha Forrest and fell dead from a bullet in his brain.

****

"Boss! Our boy out in Decatur got hit!" Convict said excitedly as he rushed into Cam's office.

"Surprised he lasted this long," Cam mumbled to himself. The news wasn't new since Anthony had already filled him in. Hiring the young cop had proven to be a wise move. Now he had an inside scoop on everything the cops knew. "So, who gonna take his place out there?"

"Ced on it. I got the security video from the motel," he said, loading the disc into the computer on Cam's desk.

"What the fuck..." Cam reeled when he saw Cameisha and Bad Ass enter the room. The quick flash from the gunshot could be seen through the curtains.

"I'll put Milsap an' 'em on them and..." Convict started until Cam interrupted him.

"No need. She'll come to me," he said knowingly. What he couldn't understand was what she was doing back in the country. He knew she'd made it safely to South America and had millions to live on. He watched the footage again and asked, "What are you doing here?"

****

"Okay. Um..." Big Shawn stammered when Cam answered his call. There really was no nice way to say what he had to say so he just said it. "Your daughter just bought a gun to kill you. I don't think she knows it's you, but she said she's going to kill the owner of Club Illusions."

"And you sold it to her?" Cam asked incredulously.

"Yeah, along with a box of blanks," he replied.

"Thanks for the heads up," he said and hung up. He would have his answer in a few hours. He turned to his guest and said, "Guess what?"

****

"Ooh-ooh-owe-ooh-ouch," Cameisha fussed as she gently inserted the small pistol inside of her. It may be small but it was metal and still shaped like a gun and guns were not made to go in vaginas.

Cameisha had been by the club a few times that day to scope it out. She knew where to park so she could do the hit and hit the backdoor. She thought about catching him at the end of the night but decided that it would be easier to get him in his office.

After parking the getaway car, she pulled up to the valet in a bor-rowed car. Technically, it was stolen, but she borrowed it from the car thief.

"Welcome to Club Illusions," a burly female bouncer greeted. She gave an intense stare into Cameisha's eyes to see if she needed a stud in her life.

"Thank you," she replied and raised her arms so the woman could scan her with a wand.

"This girl has balls. Huge balls," Cam said as he watched via the security monitors.

"Um...?" the bouncer asked as the wand beeped as it passed over the front of Cameisha's crotch. All kind of freaky thoughts ran through the stud's man as to what it could be. Maybe she had a golden coochie, or platinum, even.

"I got a gun in my coochie," Cameisha spat sarcastically. The bouncer began to protest until she heard her boss in her earpiece.

"Let her in," Cam instructed without further explanation.

"Thank you. Have fun," the stud said, stepping aside to let her enter. She ran her eyes up and down Cameisha's body as she sashayed on into the club.

"Hey," Meisha sang as she walked in to hear her jam playing. She put a little wiggle in her walk as she moved through the club. She made her way to the bar but the gun inside of her made it too hard to climb onto the bar stool.

Cameisha pictured her and her girls in the club turning up and turning down the players and macks who tried to crack. She remembered what she came for and focused. The office was up a flight of steps being guarded by either a huge man or someone had put a suit on a gorilla. Her mind scrambled on different ways to get around, over or under him to get to the stairs.

"Should've brought a banana," she thought to herself.

Suddenly, the man put a finger in his free ear to hear the earpiece in the other one. He nodded as if he speaker could see him and walked away.

Cameisha wasted no time and hastily moved forward. She ascended the stairs as quickly as the gun in her box would allow. When she reached the owner's office, she pressed her ear to the door. At the same time, she opened her legs, pulled her panties to the side and gently pulled out the pistol. She went to take it off safety and realized that she'd never put the safety on.

"Oh wow," she muttered and shook her head. "Trigga would be mad if I blew up the coochie."

It took a quick pep talk to urge herself on. She had gotten herself in a real jam and had to get herself out. The man behind the door had to die so her family could live. The door opened quietly and she raised the gun. The man had his back to her as he looked out the window at the Atlanta skyline. She doubted the veracity of the tiny gun and crept forward to get as close as she could. She knew it was fucked up to murder the man like this but he was in her way. She got right behind him and pointed at his medulla oblongata.

"Sorry, no hard feelings," she offered and pulled the trigger. The little gun had a loud bark but no bite. The man didn't even flinch, let alone drop dead. She stepped forward and fired again.

"Blanks," Cam laughed as he turned.

Cameisha nearly had a heart attack when she saw him.

"Yeah, now come give me a hug!" he insisted and threw his arms open.

She ran and slammed into him. "I'm so glad I didn't kill you," she said and broke down at the thought.

"I'm glad my nigga Bigs put blanks in the gun. Now..." he said, separating himself so he could look at her. "Why are you here? Why did you kill my man out in Decatur? What's going on?"

"It's a long story. *Dope Girl 5*, actually," she sighed.

He led her over to the sofa and they sat as she laid it all out. Cam fought the urge to smile at the gangsta ass story. "So, why didn't you just say something?" he asked while sending out a text.

"To who? Besides, this Sosa got people at grandma's house with my baby! He got the phone tapped, bank account frozen..."

"Guess I gotta go pay this Sosa dude a visit!" Cam growled.

"Daddy, ain't no way you can take on all them people alone!" she exclaimed, sounding like the little country girl he met years ago.

"He's not alone," her favorite uncle said as he walked in on the conversation.

"Killa!" she screamed and rushed over to hug him.

Cam blushed and turned his head when her dress rose above her ass from jumping on Killa.

Chapter 25

Cameisha looked back and forth between her father and uncle as they plotted out a plan to save their family. This would be a dream come true to bang it out with Killa and Cam. However, it was not to be.

"Let me come, Daddy! I bust my gun, too! Tell 'em, Unc!" she urged Killa to co-sign.

"The girl will bust something," he agreed with a nod. "Remember E-Man?"

"No! How 'bout them dudes from Nelson? I aired that shit out!" she cheered. They high fived while Cam looked on like *really*.

"Nah. Besides, you gotta meet Sosa with that shipment. I want that work along with his head. Convict will stay here with you."

"Oh, okay," she pouted and gave up. She had plans for that work, too. It's the curse of being a hustler. Once a dope girl, always a dope girl.

****

Michelle looked at her husband between her chocolate thighs and wondered what he was up to. He was eating the pussy like a taco salad but there was something else to it. He was up to something or he wanted something. A vicious orgasm interrupted her thoughts. She came so hard that she let out a howl that echoed up in the vaulted ceiling.

She knew he definitely wanted something when he flipped her on her side and lifted up her leg. He lined up his dick and plunged inside. When he reached the bottom, she decided he could have whatever he wanted. She grabbed fistfuls of the silk sheets and held on while he pounded away.

"Shit!" Cam fussed as he felt a tingle in his toes. He knew that it would spread throughout his body and explode out of his dick. It wasn't a bad thing but he wanted her to cum first. He got his wish a few strokes later when his wife howled once more. He let go right behind her.

"Yes. Sure. Okay, honey," she said after recovering from the good nut. Partially, anyway, since her leg was still shaking.

"Yes, what?" he asked with a perplexed smile.

"Yes to whatever that was about. Aren't you about to ask or tell me something?" she asked knowingly. It was just another reminder to Cam that she was his soulmate.

"No, I mean yes...well... I gotta go outta town. Got business."

"Okay," she said since she'd already agreed. "I'll be right here when you get back."

"Mmmm," he said, feeling her squeeze her vagina around his deflated dick. He used sheer willpower to make it hard again.

They switched to the missionary position so they could fuck face to face. A going away present for both of them.

****

"Here's the plan," Meisha said once she had Self and Bad Ass assembled. "My daddy finna murk this Sosa nigga before he get to America. The shipment is already in motion, so we gonna jack it!"

"Okay, I got one question," Little Self asked, raising his hand.

"Shoot, my nigga!" Cameisha barked just like her daddy did when he held court with his cronies.

"Yeah...um...are you crazy? You want us, me and him to rob some Columbian drug lord?" he asked, making it sound as crazy as it was.

Cameisha couldn't hear it, though, because her ears were filled with her own ego. "That's two questions," the smart aleck quipped. "Yes, to both and they're Brazilian, not Columbian. Yo, B, if this shit pop off, we gon' be rich as fuck!"

"I'm down!" Bad Ass agreed. No surprise since he was always with the bullshit. "Yo, son, quicker we get this money, the quicker you can bounce with yo' girl."

"I guess," he agreed half-heartedly. "I guess."

****

"You look sleepy, son," Killa said when Cam met him at the airport.

"Drained is more like it," he said.

Michelle tried to get a week's worth of dick in one night. She was back home curled up in their bed like a ball while he was off to South America. He, too, went to sleep once he got seated on the plane. He was jolted awake when they landed in Brazil.

One of Killa's contacts met their plane to take them to a safe house. He had guns, clothes and cars on standby. Plus, he could get them whatever else they requested at the drop of a dime.

"Gocho!" Killa said, embracing his close friend. "This is my cousin, Cameron Forrest. Cam, my pa'tner, Gocho."

The two strangers shook and become friends. He led them through the airport to his car and drove them into the city. He played the perfect host, pointing out landmarks and tourist attractions as they rode. Once they reached the house, it was time to get to business.

"Tell us about this Sosa," Cam began.

Gocho immediately frowned upon hearing the name. "An animal. He has no honor. He was supplying The United States through the Salazar family. Unfortunately, they all perished from a suicide bombing at a funeral."

"That shit was so gangsta!" Killa interrupted, sounding like a groupie.

"She got that shit from me! Well, my pops!" Cam shot back proudly.

"Son, your pops got that from me! I blew up a funeral way back in the day," Killa returned. They volleyed back and forth while Gocho looked on in disbelief.

"My bad, go 'head and finish what you was saying," Cam offered.

"Um..." Gocho said, trying to remember where he'd left off. "Oh yeah, he has no honor. He will still kill your people once he gets what he wants."

"He's not going to live long enough to kill nothing!" Killa growled. "He has no honor and I have no chill! Where can we find him?"

"Like you said, a funeral. Where does his mother live?" Cam wanted to know.

"I'll show you tomorrow. Tonight, let's hit the club!"

****

Brazil may be the home of the biggest Jesus statue in the world but that obviously meant nothing because it was also one of the most licentious places on the planet. When night fell, the streets were lined, on both sides, with prostitutes of every kind.

There were blondes and brunettes, red heads and dread heads. There were white, black, tall short, skinny and thick women. There were fuck-men for men who fucked men and kids for the sickest of society.

"Me and my girl gonna have to come see about this shit!" Killa said, seeing a little girl dressed like a grown whore. It reminded him of those beauty pageants they have for little girls back in the States. He could literally feel his blood begin to boil.

"She is one of those children advocates?" Gocho asked.

"Nah, she's a lunatic that hates shit like this!" he replied.

Sosa owned the club they were heading to. They hoped to get a glimpse of the elusive leader even though getting next to him would be next to impossible.

"Shit!" Killa and Cam said in unison as they entered the club. A naked woman was perched on a pedestal spread eagle with another woman lapping at her vagina. On the other side, there was a woman pleasuring a man in the same manner.

"I may need to rethink ladies' night at my spot," Cam said. "Or not."

"Speak of the devil," Gocho said once they were seated. He nodded up to the VIP section. All eyes peered through the dim light and thick smoke for a glimpse of the man.

A beautiful, black Brazilian girl with natural hair kneeled in front of him and blew him while he laughed, drank and spoke to his comrades.

"He sure knows how to party," Killa commented. Dancers were dancing on the dance floor but several sex acts took place openly throughout the club.

Cam focused on his target, burning the man's face into his memory. He came and left through a back door flanked by bodyguards. He would not be easy to get to.

"Let's bounce," Cam suggested once Sosa departed. Not to mention all the sex and sexy women were starting to get to him. Brazil was known for having one of the highest HIV rates in the world so he wouldn't touch anything there even if he wasn't married.

"Yeah, let me get my girl on the line. She got a mean phone sex game," Killa agreed as he stood.

"Phone sex?" Cam wondered. "How does that work?"

"That's a bit personal, cuz," Killa laughed. He still gave him a few pointers as they rode back to the house. Once they arrived, they parted ways as they retired to their rooms where they both grabbed their phones and called their women.

"Is everything okay?" Michelle asked of the late night video call when she answered. She fluffed her hair to look good for husband. It wasn't needed since he wasn't calling to speak to her anyway.

"Put your coochie on the phone!" he demanded in a rush.

"What? You so nasty!" she smiled wickedly. She let the camera slowly scan down her body. By the time it reached her wonderful black box between her legs, she was super wet.

Cam squirted some lotion into his palm and got to work. No mystery how things ended.

Chapter 26

None of Sosa's family members had passed so Cam and Killa decided to murder one. They assumed his beloved mother's funeral would make for the biggest turn out and set their sights on her.

They knew if they put a bullet in her head, it would bring too much heat and that the funeral would have an army in attendance for a murder so they settled on an accident. Actually, Killa was going to run her off the road.

"Here she comes," Cam radioed when he saw the old woman's Benz leave its gated estate.

"I'm on her," Killa announced as he pulled out behind her. The road leading to town was so curved and crooked that he held on tightly to the steering wheel. She was nearing the village so he had to make his move before it was too late.

"Son of a bitch!" the old lady fussed in Portuguese when Killa bumped her from behind. She lifted a hand a shoot him the bird but he bumped her again. She would have to save the bird for the devil when she got to hell because the last bump sent her barreling over the cliff.

"As my girl would say...'Okay, bye-bye,'" Killa cracked up as he watched the car bouncing down the cliff in his rearview mirror. He pouted in disappointment when it didn't explode. "Aww, man!"

****

"What? When? How?" Sosa barked in response to the news of his mother's death. His response was fake as fuck since he'd been waiting for the old broad to croak. Now he could move into the family's lavish villa and have it all to himself.

His plan was to fill it with exotic beauties of all races, colors and nationalities. He planned to get head in every language on the globe. He did not plan on buying a stitch of clothing for any of them. Instead, they'd have to run around naked. There'd be Chinese, East and West Indians, Eskimos and Asians. Oh, and he'd have a cute and sassy little black girl named Cameisha after he killed her family.

"I will make all the arrangements," his uncle assured him.

"Arrangements? Arrangements for what?" Sosa asked. His mind had drifted to visions of naked women at his pool.

"For the funeral. Don't worry, her remains are safe at the funeral home," he replied. "All you will have to do is come. It would be nice for you to give the eulogy."

"Huh? Yeah, yeah, sure," he lied once more. He was headed to America. He had a drug deal to make. Once he got Cameisha's network of dealers, he would kill her family and take her back to Brazil and keep her butt naked by the pool.

****

Killa and Cam had to prepare for the funeral as well, even though neither planned on attending it. When nightfall came, they snuck down to the funeral home and broke in. Business was obviously good according to the back room full of bodies waiting to be planted.

"You probably need to let me handle this part on my own. Just guard the door and make sure no one is coming," Killa offered once they reached the bodies.

"Shawty, I can handle anything you can handle," Cam shot back. The two had become as close as brothers and that made them highly competitive.

"If you say so," Killa shrugged and lifted a sheet off a corpse. The head lay next to the torso but its missing fingers were in sight. They were up his ass but they had no reason to look there.

"Guess he couldn't count," Cam chuckled. He knew the best way to deal with sticky fingers was to cut them off.

"Damn, I wonder what she did," Killa said, seeing the pretty black girl from the other night at the club. The ligature marks around her slender neck suggested that she'd been strangled. Both men grew silent in their rage.

A lumpy mass of flesh under a nearby sheet proved to be the late Mrs. Sosa. They both scrunched their faces at the sight of the naked eighty-year-old. Even eighty-year-old men don't want to see that. A hundred-year-old maybe, but definitely not the two thirty-something-year-old cousins.

"Wh-wh-wh-what are y-you doing?" Cam stammered as Killa produced a scalpel and cut the stitches holding her chest cavity closed from the autopsy.

"I t-t-t-told you," he snickered and began stuffing her chest cavity with explosives. "Like my girl always says, it's just like preparing chicken."

"I really need to meet this Yolo," Cam said. He was definitely intrigued by and anxious to meet the woman who had his cousin's nose open.

Cam tried to avert his eyes from the woman's empty insides. He looked down but the eighty-year-old's vagina forced his eyes back up. He watched Killa connect blasting caps to the high powered explosives before he finally gingerly hooked it to a cell phone and powered it on.

"Whew!" Killa exclaimed when they didn't blow up. "I always get the wires confused. I just close my eyes and pick eenie, meenie, minie, moe."

"Bruh?" Cam said in disbelief.

"Just kidding! This is what I do! Now, as soon as we dial this number, it's *hello from the other side,*" he sang.

****

"Paper!" Killa called out to Cam's scissors. Everyone knows that scissors cuts paper, so Cam won.

"Yes!" he cheered and pumped his fist. What he won was the honor of pressing send on the cell phone that would send the current to the blasting caps which, in turn, would send Sosa and his entire family to whatever they had coming in the afterlife, be it the hellfire or Paradise.

"Let's flip for it!" Killa pouted. After all, it was what he did.

"Heads!" Cam called out cheered again when he won again.

"Whatever. I'll head over to keep eyes on the clan. You can make the call from grandma's house," he conceded.

The cousins departed with a pound and went on to their separate missions. Cam found a spot near his grandmother's house so he could watch the guards who guarded the family. Killa went and found a spot a safe distance away from the funeral home. As soon as Sosa walked in, he'd call his cousin to make the call to detonate the device. Once he was in place, he called to check in.

"How's it looking over there?" he asked Cam as more people pulled up to the funeral home.

"Gravy! They've all left, except for one," he replied. The others had left to pay their respects to the old lady.

"It's filling up over here. Everyone is here already, except Sosa! Just waiting on... Shit!" Killa fussed.

"What?" Cam asked urgently. "Is everything okay?"

"No! They just pulled the carriage around. Once they move the body we're fucked!"

"What do you want me to do?"

"Blow it! Fuck it, we'll catch him later," Killa relented.

Cam pressed the send button but was too far away to see or her the results. All he heard was a roar in the cell phone and his cousin cheer.

"Wow!" Killa clapped, smiling at the display. The windows and doors were all blown out, spewing body parts out on to the street.

"What happened? Did it work?" Cam asked eagerly.

"Yooooo!!! That shit was dope!" Killa rubbed it in. He didn't get to press the button but at least he got to see it.

They both clicked off and sprang into action. Killa headed over to the bank while Cam moved to save his family. Cam hopped out of the car dressed like a beggar. The disguise allowed him to walk right up to the guard.

The guard got on guard when he saw him then relaxed when he saw the tattered clothing of the beggar. Cans rattled in the burlap sack he had slung over his shoulder.

"Come!" the man ordered, intending to do his good deed for the day. He wrapped up the uneaten half of sandwich from his lunch to give to the beggar. He heard the cans rattled louder as Cam dug inside the sack. He looked up just in time to see the flash that sent him off to the next life.

"Killa's here!" Grandma Diedra cheered and clapped upon hearing the gunshot. Sincerity and Trigga had tried to keep her in the dark about the siege but the old lady had been thuggin' since before either of them was thought of.

"'Bout time!" Sincerity fussed. Not only was she ready to be rescued but her lonely vagina needed some attention, too. To everyone's surprise, it was Killer Cam not Killa who walked into the house.

"Cameron! Where's Xavier?" Diedra asked as she hugged the shit out of him. She released him a split second before he passed out.

"He had to stop by the bank. He's going to meet us at the airport. Now pack what means the most to you and let's go!" Cam ordered.

****

"No!" the bank's manager said defiantly. "Sosa said... Owee!"

"This little piggy," Killa laughed as he snipped the man's pinky off. His ring finger was next when he still refused to transfer the money he had frozen. "Trust me, Sosa won't be alive long enough do to do anything about it!"

By the time that last little piggy went wee-wee-wee, the man had given up and made the transfer. He had to use his left hand since all of his fingers on the right were gone. Killa was nice enough to let him keep them after he gave up what didn't belong to him.

"Sosa will kill me when he returns from America," the man whined.

"No, he won't," Killa assured him and then killed him himself. He then quickly got Cam on the phone as he sped to reach the family at the airport.

"Yo," Cam said taking the call.

"Sosa isn't here! He's in the States!"

Chapter 27

"Okay, my dad is making me bring his partner to the meet. Spare him but make it look like you robbing us, too," Cameisha coached. The plan had changed but she wasn't about to give up. She couldn't because she was a spoiled brat.

"We dead," Self said, shaking his head. He just couldn't see things turning out well.

"Chill, B, we got this!" Bad Ass encouraged. He loved this wild cowboy shit and couldn't wait to bust his gun.

"I..." Cameisha began but was cut off by her phone. She saw the name *Daddy* on the screen and sent the call to voicemail. "Anyway..."

"Fuckin' brat!" Cam growled when he got her voicemail. He clicked off and called Convict.

"Sup, shaaaawty," he said in the slow, relaxed cadence brought on by getting some head. Juanna looked up and fluttered her eyes happily at him. It pleased her to please him.

"Bruh, where's my daughter?' he demanded.

"I'on know. We 'posed to meet in an hour to do that thing," he replied in code. He trusted his woman implicitly but still she didn't need to know the details of what he did.

"Where? What time?" Cam practically shouted. "Sosa is in the States! We just landed in Miami and the next flight to Atlanta doesn't leave for an hour!"

Convict reluctantly stopped his girl's bobbing head so he could focus. He stepped out of the room to so that he could speak freely and gave him the details of the meet. Little did he know but the plans were being changed as they spoke. Cam was planning, too, and called Anthony.

****

123

"Sosa! What are you doing here?" Carlos asked when the boss arrived at the dock. They were packing the shipment of coke to take to Cameisha for distribution.

"Making sure that I don't lose my investment!" he barked as he inspected the shipment. "Take it to the stash house."

"But, boss...we're supposed to meet..." Carlos began and stopped when he received a Venus Williams backhand hit to the mouth. If Sosa ever decided to be a pimp, he'd definitely have a head start because his pimp slap was down pat. Men don't like getting slapped once, let alone twice, so Carlos didn't risk getting slapped a second time. Instead, he followed directions as if Simon said them and redirected the drugs.

"Now what?" Carlos asked, rubbing the finger shaped welts on his cheek.

"Now go to that meeting and kill the girl. Kill them all!"

****

"How do you know this? You better not be pulling my leg! If we go there and don't find anything, it's your ass!" the chief barked at Anthony. He didn't think much of the young cop but if he nabbed the notorious Sosa, he was going to run for mayor.

"I made an arrest of a dealer who gave up the deal," Anthony lied. In truth, Cam had passed on the information to be passed on to the police. Sosa was far too dangerous to be loose in Atlanta.

The chief wasn't sure if he could take the word of the rookie but then again, he couldn't afford not to. He summoned the task force and SWAT team to make the bust.

****

Convict frowned as he read the text message from Cam. He looked into his rearview mirror and saw Self and Bad Ass doing a bad job of following him. A moment later, his phone buzzed.

"Sup, lil' mama?" he answered as instructed.

"You, big daddy," Cam laughed. "Abort the mission. Don't go anywhere near that warehouse. Take that...girl to the club and keep her there until I arrive.

"Wh-wha- Where are you going?" Cameisha demanded as he drove past the exit where the meet was supposed to take place. She figured she would never get her money back from Sosa so she needed to hit a lick to live off.

"Change of plans," Convict said smoothly. He was lucky he'd made Cameisha leave her gun because she would have pulled it on him at the moment.

"Nigga, you 'bout to blow off a multi-million-dollar deal for some ass? I'll give some ass!" she pleaded

"No, thank you," he laughed at the obvious lie. Even if it was the truth, she was too young and too pretty for his tastes. He cracked up even harder at her trying to discretely look for her partners in crime. "They still behind us."

"Who?" she said, trying to play it off but he twisted his lip like *yeah right*. "Aww, shit! My daddy back, ain't he?"

"Mm-hmm," Convict nodded and continued on towards the club.

****

Sosa looked up from the security monitor long enough to check his watch. Even though this was a setup, he still felt slighted by Cameisha being late. News of the funeral bombing had him even more eager to see the girl die.

"They are here!" Sosa's man announced when he saw lights pull up to the warehouse. What he didn't see was the SWAT team dressed in black like ninjas.

"Kill them all!" he said, leaning in closer to the monitor so that he wouldn't miss any of it. He didn't. He watched a massive gun battle destroy his small army of shooters.

In the end, all ten of his men lay dead along with two cops. No drugs were found because none had been sent. Anthony lowered his head in shame when his boss approached.

"No need to cower, you did good. This was obviously a double cross. That means Sosa and his dope are somewhere in my city. "Find them!" he ordered. The young cop opened his mouth to protest but got cut off by a wave of the captain's hand. "No excuses, find him!"

****

"That means that maniac is somewhere loose in my city!" Cam fumed. "Him and a ton of dope! That's gonna slow me up. I want them found!"

"Boss, I..." Convict began but stopped himself. He didn't take excuses himself so he wasn't going to make any. "I'm on it."

"Good, now where is my daughter?" he asked. "And those boys?"

"In your office," he replied as Cam marched off in that direction. "Glad I ain't her!"

"Daddy, I..." Cameisha began. She had come up with a tale to explain but he wasn't hearing it.

"Daddy nothing," he said and clicked on the TV. The deadly raid was the top story. They watched in silence while realizing just how close they'd come to dying today.

"And you two were going to rob them with a Mac and a Chopper!" Cam laughed at Self and Bad Ass. They both lowered their heads from the sting of being laughed at. Once he was done with them, he turned back to her. "I'm taking you to the airport! Killa will meet you in Belize and take you to the house. Don't come back!"

"Okay," Cameisha whined in defeat, realizing that she had already used eight of her nine lives. It was time to lay it down. No more dope girl. "What about my money? Aqua? My brothers?"

"Your uncle has your money. You got a cool million waiting on you in Belize."

"A million! I had eight!" she protested like it was really hers.

"And now you got one! Leave it to you and that would've been gone, too! Rolexes for everyone," he teased. "I'll send your buddy and her son down to you. I got these two as well."

Self gulped loudly wondering what he meant. They shared a teary eyed good-bye with their big sister. Everyone knew they would never see each again. Even Cam was moved by the touching display.

"Okay, okay, she got a plane to catch. Y'all lil' niggas hang out here until I get back," he said and led Cameisha away.

Chapter 28

"What?" Cam asked, feeling Convict staring at him from his side. It was unusual for him to smoke weed but tonight he was taking huge pulls off a large joint.

"That was cool what you did," he admired.

Cam had spent a big chunk of money getting Self and Bad setup out West. He knew they weren't responsible enough to pay rent so he paid cash for their homes, their cars and their barbershop so they couldn't fuck up. He even broke them off enough cash to keep them going for a while.

"You think them lil' niggas gon' make it?" Convict wondered.

"Fifty-fifty," Cam surmised. "They both got good in 'em and bad. Just depends which side wins."

"If the bad side wins, that would make one hell of a book!"

Cam also spread money around to each of his real and adopted children. Everyone got a million-dollar trust fund to jump start their lives. Life was good except for one major problem.

"We gotta find this fuckin' Sosa!" Cam said and took another drag off the spliff.

"I got my ear to the street. Ain't none of that dope touched yet, but when it do, we'll know about it!"

****

"I love this country!" Sosa announced as he watched the two young girls bobbing below. He popped another Viagra and washed it down with cognac.

"Boss, we are not in our country," Carlos warned. He knew his boss was violent as he was freaky, and he was plenty freaky. Not only was he on the hunt for a distributor for his product but also concubines for his villa.

He held cocaine fueled orgies every night as auditions. The freaky young black woman who was currently on her knees in front of him gagged on his dick, getting his full attention. She gagged again, making it sound even louder when he skeeted on her tonsils.

"Mmm," she moaned as she milked him dry. Once she finished swallowing, she smiled up at him.

"What is your name?" he demanded.

She had just sucked her way to an all-expense paid trip to Brazil. The only drawback was getting murdered and dumped like garbage when he was done with her.

"Britney," she replied with a smile on her face and cum on her breath. She ducked her head and went for seconds. She didn't make the Olympics but she was going to Brazil.

"Boss, our guests have arrived. Perhaps it would be best if you put that, away," Carlos suggested. He was right, too, because no man wants to walk in on a business meeting and see another man's penis.

"She almost won gold," Sosa chuckled as he lifted Britney's head. "Wait in my room. Carlos will take you home soon."

"Okay," Britney and the white girl named Sarah sang and skipped off naked. The doorbell chimed and Carlos set off to open the door.

"Sup, shawty," a local dealer called Havoc greeted. He extended his hand like the gentlemen he was not. He was on his best behavior for this meeting. If this connect had access to the kind of weight he said he did, then he'd be rich instead of just acting it.

It was his acting rich in a club that had gotten him noticed by Carlos. The mid-level dealer had been popping bottles and putting on in the VIP section of a club. Carlos made his pitch and here they were.

"Uh...yes...thanks for coming," Carlos replied. He now doubted the man after seeing him in the light of day. He looked more like a common street thug than a boss. "Follow me."

"Nice crib," Havoc admired as he followed Carlos into the den where Sosa waited.

"How much product can you handle? What do you move each day?" Sosa demanded off the top. He was ready to get his done so he could get back to the girls in his room.

"Shawty, I got my city on smash!" Havoc exaggerated. He did have his Westside projects on lock but it would take a lot more territory than that to move the kind of weight Sosa was talking about.

"So...one hundred kilos a week? Two?" he demanded.

"A hunned!" Havoc nearly choked. He suddenly realized he was in over his head, but couldn't let this opportunity slip by. Having an overseas connect was every dope boy's dream. "No problem. What's the ticket?"

"Fifteen. I expect one-point-five seven days from today."

"O-o-ok-k-kay," he stammered. It was literally time to get rich or die trying.

****

"Gurl, look!" Britney exclaimed at a gold watch sitting on the dresser. It was so heavy that she let out a grunt when she picked it up.

"Un huh. Ooooh, loo'!" Sarah said like the ghetto girl she wasn't. She clipped her words and added extra sass to sound black. On the phone, one would swear she was Shontay, not Sarah. Either way, the pearl handle .45 caliber pistol on the nightstand spoke for itself.

"Girl, I ain't worried 'bout him. I got him sprung," she said and cuffed the watch.

"Where were we?" Sosa asked as he rushed into the bedroom.

"Right here!" Britney announced and opened her mouth wide. "Aaaaah."

After spending several hours exploring the girls' orifices, Sosa summoned Carlos, who wasn't pleased to be reduced to driver and butler, to take them home. The sooner Sosa went home, the better.

"Addresses!" Carlos barked at the girls in the backseat. He entered both into the car's GPS to plot their routes. Britney's house was closer so it was their first stop. That worked great for Sarah.

"Can I tell you something?" Sarah asked the second that Britney got out of the car.

"What?" he snapped. He made sure to be harsh so she wouldn't try to offer him any sexual favors.

"My friend stole a watch from the bedroom. Oh, and a diamond ring," she said, adding her theft to Britney's crime as well.

"I see," Carlos nodded and looked at the address displayed on the GPS.

Chapter 29

"Boss, we missing a ton of money out there!" Convict said, contradicting Cam's decision to pull all the work off the streets.

"We ain't gon' starve," Cam replied. The club's business was booming so they were still eating well. He knew that a good drought would bring Sosa and his shipment of coke out of hiding.

"Nah, but we could be killing the game right now!" he stressed. Greed was audible in his voice and Cam heard it loud and clear.

"Greed will make you rich or dead, and you don't get to choose which," he warned. Just like the saying you can lead a horse to water but can't make him drink, you can give sincere advice but you can't make a person heed it.

"Aight, boss. I'ma keep my ear to the street and see what's poppin'," Convict said. They exchanged a pound and off he went.

"Daddy?" Kayla called in a second before opening his office door and inviting herself in.

"Come on in," he said sarcastically towards the door as if she were still behind it.

"Anyway," she giggled on her way around to his desk. He looked at her curiously as she laid out the club's ledgers on his desk. "Someone's stealing!"

Cam followed her line for line and sure enough, the numbers were off. Clubs are cash businesses and nothing sticks to sticky fingers like cash. Kayla was on the job and had easily traced the theft to user nineteen.

"Who is user nineteen?" he wondered, twisting his lips as if it would help him figure it out.

Luckily, his daughter was on top of things. "That new guy! Rodney!" she fussed with a hand on her hip. The gesture was so much like her late mother that it froze Cam in place for a moment. "Daddy?"

"Huh? Yes," he asked when she bought him back to the present.

"I said, it's Rodney! Oh, and he tried to talk to me!"

"About what?" Cam asked. He felt silly as soon as he heard it. "Okay. I'm on it."

"You want me to fire his ass? Cuz I don't mind!"

"I got it, baby. Thank you."

Kayla didn't understand the extra he put on the hug but enjoyed it none the less. It was great having her daddy back. "You're welcome," she cheered and skipped happily from his office.

As soon as she left, he went to his security system. He pulled up footage from the previous night and watched as Rodney skimmed money all night long. He started stealing the money from every fourth sale. An hour later, he started splitting it fifty/fifty with the club.

"Oh, so you just said fuck me, huh?" Cam asked the image on the footage as he watched him stole every dime he touched during the last hour. "You got it backwards, shawty... It's fuck you!"

****

"Mmhm, I see you," Convict said while he and Cam watched Rodney, live and in person, as he ran his personal Go-Fund-Me account from the bar.

"Told you," Cam replied. At the moment, he was operating a two for one in favor of the club.

"I'm finna drag this nigga out back and..."

"Kill him? Nah, too primitive," Cam laughed wickedly. "I got something else in mind."

"Cool. I'ma go get a drank," he said and headed up to the VIP section. There was a table that was always reserved for Cam but since he was in the office, he had it all to himself.

"Hey, Convict, what can I get you?" the waitress asked, even though she knew the answer. She mouthed the word *cognac* along with him and giggled.

Convict watched the woman's ass shift as she walked away. More out of curiosity than lust since it was head week at home and he couldn't wait to get home. His eyes made it over to Rodney until his drink came.

"I should buy the bar out in this bitch! I got money fo' real," a loud-mouth bragged from the next table. The gaudy jewelry dangling from his neck was some of the flea market's finest and his suit was obviously straight off the rack.

Convict was ready to dismiss him as another loudmouth with a decent trap. The type that buys a suit and think he's ready for the big leagues. His next sentence, however, got Convict's full attention.

"I got that work!" he told the groupies flanking him. "We getting it skraight from across the water. They fronting me as much as I want!"

"Sho-nuff!" Convict said to himself and leaned in closer to listen. There was no charge for the drink but he shoved a hundred-dollar bill at the waitress. She opened her mouth to thank him but got shushed so he could her the loudmouth. Ten minutes in, he said the golden words.

"Sosa got that shit by the boatload!" he vowed.

Convict had heard enough so he made his way over. "'Scuse me, shawty," he said politely, causing all eyes to turn to him. "I couldn't help but hear you say you had a plug."

"Hell yeah!" the loudmouth replied loudly. He then spent the next hour telling him all of his business. A minute after he finished, Convict rushed into Cam's office.

"Our boy is up to 'one for us, two for him," Cam said, shaking his head.

"And I found Sosa!"

****

"Britney!" Mrs. Thompson shouted down the hall. She knew if her daughter was home that she would be sleeping. That's all she did when she was there. Shower, change clothes and rest between abortions every ten months. "Britney!"

"What? What? What?" the young woman shouted back. She had the nerve to be upset with the woman who not only raised her but her children as well. Not only was her mama yelling but a car was also outside honking.

"Chile, you better check yo' tone! I know that! And one of your...friends is laying on his horn in my driveway!"

"Why it gotta be one of my friends? How you know it ain't one of your damn friends?"

"Cuz my pussy ain't got no drive-thru!" she shot back. "Now, go tell him to stop blowing that damn horn in front of my damn house!"

"Can't wait to get up out this bitch!" Britney mumbled to herself as she rolled out of the bed. Her children glared at her without speaking and she didn't speak, either. She was tired, hungover and in no mood to deal with any kids.

"Here she comes, boss!" Carlos announced when Britney staggered outside.

She squinted in the light of day like a person who hadn't seen it in a while. That's because she hadn't. The party girl partied by night and slept by day. Evidence of her heavy duty partying was beginning to show. She had dark rings under her bloodshot eyes and her skin was pale from lack of sunlight.

"Sup?" Britney croaked. She'd wanted to sound sexy but her voice was dry and harsh from turning up. She cleared her throat and tried it again. "Hey y'all. I thought y'all was coming later tonight."

"Get in!" Sosa demanded. She hopped in and saw his exposed penis sticking out through his expensive slacks. She didn't need to be told once, let alone twice, what to do.

"Mmm," Britney moaned as she felt his flaccid penis inflate inside her mouth. By the time Carlos pulled away from her mother's subdivision, she was working his full erection with her lips and hands.

"This was all you had to do to be taken care of," Sosa said, stroking her hair. The tenderness only lasted for a second before he snapped. He grabbed her head forcefully and shoved it down his cock until she gagged. "You steal from me!"

"Boss, let's wait until we get to the house," Carlos pleaded as the girl began to struggle.

"Steal from me!" he shouted again as he viciously fucked her face.

Britney gagged and fought for her life. No one wants their cause of death to be dick inhalation so she clamped down.

Sosa wrapped an arm around her neck and squeezed. Squeezed until she stopped biting. Squeezed until she was clawing at his forearms, drawing blood and flesh. Squeezed until she passed out and her body went limp. Squeezed until her soul slipped from her body.

"What are you doing?" Carlos shouted when Sosa opened the door as they sped along the highway. He got his answer when he shoved Britney's empty shell out of the car.

"Now I need me another black girl for my collection," he fussed.

****

"'Nother month like this and I'ma have that Beamer!" Rodney cheered as he counted cash. His take for the night was close to fifteen hundred bucks.

Being the show off that he was, he decided to floss a little bit. He pulled out his stash of stolen loot and piled it high on his coffee table. His plan was to post a few pictures to his social media pages, but others had other plans.

"Huh?" Rodney exclaimed when his door flew open from a well-placed kick. Convict stormed in with a gun in hand and Cam was right behind him with something far more ominous in his hand. "Wh-wh-what you guys doing here?"

"Damn!" Convict shouted at the sight of all the money on the table. "That's from tonight?"

"Nah, he been saving up," Cam replied. "What you hit for tonight, thirteen, fourteen hundred?"

"Fifteen and some-... Wait, I don't know what you talking about! I..." Rodney paused as Cam loaded a disk into his DVD player.

"Nice TV. 4K?" Cam asked of the curved, high definition TV his money had paid for. On it was a crystal clear image of Rodney stealing money from the club.

"It is!" Convict answered. "3D?"

"Um..." Rodney wondered over their wonder of his TV.

"Oh, my bad. Anyway, what's it going to be? Police or the hand?" Cam asked while explaining the machete in his hand at the same time.

"Please don't call the police! I got three strikes already! Next felony, they gon' give me life!" he pleaded.

"So, the hand then?" Cam asked to be sure.

"I ain't got no other choice?" the man pleaded. He wanted to keep both his hand and his freedom.

"Yup," Convict answered and racked his pistol. "Plan C."

"Bruh, you decided to live a life of crime, now you gotta take what come with it!" Cam said, running out of patience. "So, what's it going to be, the cops or the hand?"

"Mannnnn!" Rodney whined and stretched out his hand on the table.

He expected some dialog or warning but got none. Instead, Cam swung the blade like an executioner and lopped off his hand. Rodney opened his mouth to scream but it was so high pitched that it was inaudible.

"Come here, nigga!" Convict fussed and applied a tourniquet to his wrist so he wouldn't bleed to death. Cam took the opportunity to collect his stolen cash.

"Now take your dumb ass and your hand over to Grady Hospital so they can put it back on. Hurry up, too, cuz I expect you back at work in a week," he said over shoulder.

"Yeah!" Convict co-signed as he followed him out.

Chapter 30

Cam realized he was awake before he decided to open his eyes. He laid there feeling the warmth of his wife beside him. His erection throbbed to get his attention, letting him know that it needed to be relieved one way or another. He put two and two together and nudged Michelle.

"Baby, you woke?" he asked while waking her up.

"Mmhmm," she said with a stretch and a yawn. She figured he wanted some pussy before breakfast so she rolled over to give him some. He was a good husband so he could have that good pussy anytime he wanted it.

"Good morning," he drawled as he rolled on top of her. He was planting the first of what would be many kisses when his phone rang. The ringtone assigned to Mrs. Thompson playing caused him to look at the clock. Any other time, at a time like this, the call would have been ignored. However, for the caller to be calling this early was out of the norm so he took the call.

"They killed her! They killed my child last night!" Mrs. Thompson wailed. Cam felt a stab of conscious since it was he who had had her first child killed.

"Who?" he croaked as he rolled back off his wife and sat up. She popped up as well to support her husband in whatever was distorting his face.

"Britney! They found her body on the side of the highway!" the mother yelled.

Cam recalled hearing about a body found on I-20 on the nightly news. The identification hadn't been made yet so no name had been given. Once they'd run the prints of the dead girl, her mother had been notified.

"I'm on my way," he blurted and clicked off.

"You need me to come? To do anything?" the good wife offered. She was willing to do almost anything to smooth the worry lines from his forehead.

"My kids' aunt got killed. I gotta go see what's going on," he advised, just as concerned about her worry lines. He planted a kiss on her forehead and rushed to get dressed.

****

"Oh, Cameron!" Mrs. Thompson wailed and rushed into his arms. He was uncomfortable with her pressing her body so tightly against his; especially since he'd missed his morning wake up sex.

"What happened?" he asked and pulled away before his body could react to the feel of the woman. "What the police say?"

"Somebody choked her to death and then threw her out of a moving car. She can't even have an open casket," the mother sobbed.

The scene got even sadder when Britney's kids entered the room. They hadn't shed a tear for the stranger that they called mama until their father arrived. Soon they were sharing a group hug where there wasn't a single dry eye. His children's sorrow even caused a drip to fall from Cam's eye. Once they broke off, Cam sent the kids away so that he and their grandmother could talk.

"Who she be with? What is she into?" he needed to know.

"Who she don't be with? That girl was a sack chaser. Up in every club, letting everybody in her body. Done had three abortions that I know of. She, she..."

"She gotta have at least one close friend," Cam said. He knew she did because hoes often travel in pairs.

"A white girl named... Sarah," Mrs. Thompson recalled. She'd met her once when they got stranded at a motel and she'd gone to their rescue.

"Where's Britney's phone?" he asked as he started up the stairs to her rarely used bedroom. He'd had some great nights of wild sex in that room. Then again, he'd had sex in almost every room in the house. First with Shay, then with Britney and, finally, with their mother, Mrs. Thompson.

"Don't make no sense," the mother huffed at the condition of her daughter's bedroom. Designer shoes, clothes and purses were strewn about like a tornado had hit an upscale boutique. They both searched through the rubble looking for her phone. Cam found it under a hundred-dollar blouse at the same time that the mother came up with the watch. "Oh my!"

"Oh my is right!" Cam exclaimed when he felt the weight of the solid gold watch. One look at it and he knew that it was the real deal. "This will definitely get you killed!"

"Shole will," she agreed and kept searching through the piles. Cam found her phone's charger and plugged the dead phone in. As soon as it powered up, texts from Sarah began to come in.

"WYD"

"Hit me up."

"Sosa said you stole his watch and ring."

"Sosa?" Cam frowned and cocked his head curiously. It made sense since the girl made it her mission to fuck every major and minor dope boy in the city.

"Who?" Mrs. Thompson asked.

"No one. I'm gonna see what the streets talking about."

"Find out who did this to my baby. And when you do, I want you to kill him. Kill him dead!" the grieving mother appealed.

****

"Meet me at my house," Cam ordered when Convict took his call.

"Now?" he asked, hoping not since Juanna was dancing seductively atop the bed.

SA'ID SALAAM

142 SA'ID SALAAM

"One hour," he barked since that would also give him time to get home and finish what he'd started that morning as well. He pressed end to end the call and mashed on the gas.

Michelle smiled wickedly when she heard her husband pull into their driveway. She knew he had a lot on his mind and planned to put him at ease for a little while. For as long as he could last inside the wet oven she called vagina. She propped herself ass up and face down on the bed and played in her pussy while she waited for him.

"Shit! Shit! Shit!" he exclaimed thrice when he walked in on the sight of her cumming.

"Put it in! Put it in!" she pleaded desperately as she continued to work her fingers.

Cam whipped out his wood and rushed over. She came again as he slid safely inside of her. He grabbed her ass cheeks and pulled them open so he had a clear view of the long, slow strokes he delivered. His dick turned white from the creamy coating of her cum.

"It's okay, baby, let it go," she purred when she felt his stroke grow choppy. She squeezed her hot walls to help him along. It helped and he grunted loudly as he exploded. "That's it, baby. Feel better?"

"Mmhmmm," he panted and gasped. It was pure torture pulling his meat from her creamy middle but it had to be done. He had work to do.

Across town, Convict busted a nut of his own before heading Cam's way.

****

"Congratulations!" Michelle cheered when she let Convict in with a friendly hug.

"Um...thanks," he said somewhat awkwardly.

She sensed it and left it alone.

"Sup, shawty," Cam greeted and led the way downstairs to his man cave. Once they were seated comfortably on the leather, he began. "Sosa killed someone I know. A girl. Where are you with getting next to him?"

"I done shopped with his man Havoc a couple times. Ten bricks at one time. Say the word and I'll push the buy up to a hun'ed and demand a meet."

"I'll front the cash," Cam said, even though he stood the chance of losing it. One-point-five-million is not chump change.

"Bet. I'll set it up," Convict agreed. "And when dude show, I'ma pop his top."

"Or me," Cam offered. It was personal now so he wanted to handle it personally. "So...what you doing with all that extra bread you making?"

"Huh?" he asked since he was keeping what he made in the streets off the Sosa dope.

"Un huh," Cam laughed since he would have done the same. It kept the supply lines open so he could move the rest of his drugs when the time came. "So, um...what Michelle congratulating you 'bout?"

"Uh... Cuz... Um... Juanna told her I...we... I mean... 'bout to get married, shawty," he finally fessed up.

"That's what's up! Why you ain't tell me?" he cheered and asked.

"Cuz um...you know... Juanna used to be...you know... She..."

Cam wondered where he was going as he played word search in his head. Words like ugly came to mind.

"She was... You know... A hoe. People say you can't turn a hoe into a housewife but she..."

"They right. You can't turn a hoe into a housewife, but she can! If she turned into a hoe, she can turn back!" Cam insisted and he was right. It was at that moment that he understood redemption. Once a dope boy, always a dope boy was bullshit. He could be whatever he wanted to be. In fact, he was who he wanted to be; a husband, a father and a business man.

"Thanks, bruh. She a good woman, too!" Convict said happily. He thought enough of Cam to care what he thought. With his approval now in hand, he could move on.

****

"I don't know 'bout all that, shawty!" Havoc said, shaking his head no as he spoke. "The big man ain't really tryna meet nobody, ya feel me?"

"Nah, I don't. What I feel is that ain't no way in the hell I'm finna do a-million-and-a-half-dollar deal through no middle man," Convict said, sticking to his guns. His next option was to gun the man down and let his second in command take him to Sosa.

Havoc was still a small time dude but he knew enough big time dudes to move a ton of coke. Most didn't question the source as long as the quality and price were straight. He knew he could be replaced in a minute since he was just a middle man or, as Sosa referred to him, the monkey in the middle.

"He right, you know," Van whispered to his boss. His share of the million-dollar deal was more than he'd ever seen in his life. He thought about gunning the man down himself if he didn't comply. He would have to if Havoc hadn't agreed.

"Aight, shawty! I'ma hit my man up and see what he say," Havoc fussed and stormed off, leaving Convict and Van by themselves.

A brief staring contest was declared a draw when Van spoke up. "You got a number, shawty?" he smiled. Neither needed a crystal ball to see what was coming.

"Shole do!" he replied and recited his seven digits.

Chapter 31

"That her?" Convict asked of the white girl who walked into Britney's funeral. Like a typical party girl, she was underdressed for the occasion with the tattoos on the top of her tits showing.

"I'd say yes," Cam said, reading her name inked on her left breast. The other had a colorful rose cover-up that covered up the name of some long lost man who'd lost interest and moved on to the next party girl.

They both watched her as she approached the closed casket. The tears were as real as her show of grief. Part of it was grief since she was partly to blame for her being in that box. She'd wanted her spot, not her life. The weight of what she'd caused made her knees buckle.

"Whoa, lil' mama," Cam said as he caught the wobbly woman.

His kids and their grandmother glared angrily at Sarah. It wasn't her fault that Britney had become who she was but their grief needed a scapegoat. Having someone to blame can help ease the pain. Having someone to turn to and rely on eases the pain even more. Good thing God is always there.

"Thank you. I... Dang! Who is you?" she asked once she looked up at her handsome savior.

"Um," he paused to come up with a name. He looked around for one and replied, "Flowers. Tony Flowers. Were you and Britney close?"

"Best friends." Have her tell it. She then looked him up and down calculating dollar signs as she went. The two-thousand-dollar suit and ten-thousand-dollar watch spelled he had dough.

"Let's talk after the funeral," Cam suggested. He looked her up and down as well and noticed the chunky men's diamond ring hanging from a cheap gold chain around her neck.

"Who was that?" Michelle asked when Cam returned.

"A friend of Britney's," he replied and pressed his lips together tightly. It was body language for *I ain't saying nothing more on the subject.*

Cam didn't hear a word of the so-called eulogy. The preacher spoke of the young girl he'd watched grow up, not he woman she had become. Britney's mom had the calm look of a beaten woman. As if she had thrown in the towel and accepted defeat. The six sad children sitting next to her shared in her sorrow.

The ride out to the gravesite was made in quiet contemplation. Michelle was thinking about what to feed him and how to fuck him when they got home. Whatever she could do to ease the frustration etched on his face, she wanted to do.

Another speech was made and the casket was lowered into the ground. The finality of it set off another round of moans and tears. They could only pray that the tired girl would finally get some rest.

Mrs. Thompson started towards her vehicle with the kids. She stopped and separated the oldest from the youngest and marched them over to Cam. He already knew what was up before she said, "I need you to take them. I can't..."

"No problem!" Michelle blurted and opened the back door before Cam could reply.

He just shrugged his shoulders since she said what he would've said. "I'll swing by later to get their things," he advised and gave her a hug. The woman broke down in his arms and got a good cry. Her grandkids rushed over to help squeeze the tears out with a group hug.

****

"You guys make yourselves at home," Michelle told her step kids once they arrived at the house. They already had assigned rooms since they visited often anyway. "I need to speak with your dad for a few minutes."

"You do?" Cam asked and followed her up to their bedroom.

Michelle closed the door behind them and pounced. She shoved him on the bed and went for his zipper. She snatched his dick out of the expensive slacks and gave it a lick like an ice-cream cone. They both watched as it magically throbbed into full erection.

"You don't have to do..." Cam began until the head entered her hot mouth. "Never mind!"

It wasn't head week but Michelle sucked, slurped and stroked him until he exploded. She then clamped down, causing him to squirm, and gulped down all he had to offer. Only when he wet soft and limp did she eject him from her mouth.

"Feel better?" she asked. If he said no, she would go for seconds.

"I guess," he said with a weary sigh. The blowjob had taken the edge off but he still had to go kill someone today.

****

"So, what dude talking 'bout?" Cam asked when he met up with Convict.

"The meet set up for Tuesday. One hundred bricks was enough to get a meet," he replied happily. It was clear that they were headed in two different directions. Cam was looking to his exit plan while Convict was clearly a dope boy for life.

"Bruh, you do know this nigga, Havoc, is gonna cross you out, right? If you can move a hun'ed keys at a time, Sosa gon' want you on his team. That makes him obsolete."

"Oh, I know. That's why we set it up for Tuesday. Dude won't be around by then," Convict said with a murderous snarl.

"Hold that thought," Cam laughed. He pulled out a throwaway cell phone to call the throwaway white girl.

"Hello!" Sara quipped full of attitude. She even frowned up at the unknown number on her screen.

Cam had a discreet chuckle at how much she sounded like a black girl on the phone. "You wanna hang out? I got weed, pills, coke, X or whatever," Cam said, the words being the equivalent to a fisherman putting a worm on a hook.

"Who is this? Yeah, but who is this?" she snapped. Not that it mattered, since whoever it was had weed, pills, coke and X. And she planned to indulge in all of them.

"What's your address?" he asked instead of answering. She gave it and he entered it into the GPS of the throwaway phone. "I'm on my way."

"Okay," she cheered even though the call had ended. She rushed into the bathroom and under the shower. She used a dollar store douche to rinse away the semen left behind from the night before. Then she brushed her teeth and gargled for the same reason.

Cam and Convict arrived an hour later in separate cars. They parked in the parking lot of the rundown apartment complex and watched the ebb and flow of drug traffic. Blowjobs are usually for sale anywhere crack is. A few skinny crack whores scurried about like squirrels. And just like squirrels, they were trying to get nuts in their mouths.

The coast was as clear as it was going to get so Cam made his move. He was barely noticeable as he slid across the walkway dressed in all black. Convict posted up next to his car to watch the area. The gun in his hand was in case he saw something he didn't like.

"Who?" the black-white girl fussed her reply to the soft knock on her door. Cam made sure to tap softly so none of the nosey neighbors would peep out of their peepholes. He ignored the question once more so she snatched the door open. "Oh hey! I 'member you from the funeral!" she said and stepped aside so death could enter.

"Um..." Cam replied, confused by the messy apartment. It had been an hour since he'd called, yet there was still shit everywhere. Lots of party girls look like a million bucks in the club but less than zero at home.

"Excuse my place," she said as she did every time she had company. She tossed clothes from the rented sofa so they could sit. "You said something 'bout some coke."

"Yeah," he grunted and dug some out of his pocket.

Sarah lifted one end of the coffee table so all the debris could fall off. Now she had a clean surface to work. "Oh, this that butta right here!" Sarah cheered when she got her hands on the dope.

"It's aight," he said, a little jealous since it was some of Sosa's coke and not his own. He watched as she chopped, sorted then divided it into lines on the table. When she leaned over to take a snort, the diamond ring swung free from beneath her blouse. "Fucked up what happened to ole girl, huh?"

"Who?" she asked between lines. "Oh, Britney. Yeah, it is. I tol' her not to take that man's watch! He got all that coke and all them guns and she wanted to steal from him."

"Ring, too, wasn't it?" he asked, pausing her in mid-snort when he lifted the ring on the chain around her neck. "Just like this one."

"Okay, see..." she began and stopped when the choking began. She was too weak from partying to put up much of a fight. All she could do was reach for the blow for one more hit. She never made it.

"Tell Britney I sent you!" he growled and tossed the corpse on the sofa. He viciously snatched the expensive ring off the cheap chain and slid it onto his finger. It was a perfect fit, along with Sosa's watch. He searched the apartment and found his address.

"You straight?" Convict asked when Cam returned still wearing a mask of murder over his handsome face.

"Yeah. Now take that bitch to I-20 and dump her! Don't even slow down!"

Chapter 32

"I been thinking," Havoc announced, to Van's surprise.

"You have?" he asked since he wasn't known for it. He was actually known to act, react and over-react; not think.

"Yeah, shawty. If I hook ole boy up with Sosa, what Sosa gon' need me fo'?" he asked. He rubbed his neck as if he could actually feel a noose being tightened.

"Bruh, you ain't even got to worry 'bout that!" Van assured him then shot him in the temple. "See, nothing to worry 'bout."

Van packed up the cash and coke he had left and prepared to leave. He saluted the corpse on his way out as he called his new boss. If Convict was flipping a hundred bricks at a time, that's the team he needed to be on.

"Sup, shawty?" Convict drawled when he took the call. He multitasked by holding the phone with one hand while playing in Juanna's vagina with the other. His fingers were white from cum as he ran them in and out of her. She showed off by squeezing his fingers tightly and not letting them go. Van almost got hung up on.

"You and me, shawty," he confessed to murder.

"See you Tuesday. Hit me with the time and place," he said and then hung up.

Juanna rolled onto her stomach and arched her back, making her plump pussy poke out between her round ass cheeks. "Sssss," she hissed when he plunged inside. She bit down on the pillow and grabbed handfuls of the sheets as he fucked her properly. "Get...this...ssss...pussy!"

"I am!" he assured her and pounded away. The millions of dollars at his fingertips turned him on just as much as the hot pussy at the tip of his dick. He pressed down on her cervix and erupted. "Shit! Fuck! Shit!"

"Shit, fuck, shit is right," Juanna laughed. She didn't get off but was pleased to have pleased him. Besides, she'd busted a couple of good nuts during foreplay so she was content. Fair exchange ain't no robbery.

****

"Say, boss, the meet is set for..." Convict blurted as he rushed in Cam's office. He saw Anthony sitting with him and pumped his brakes. The kid was cool and all but he was still the police.

"He's cool," Cam said, urging him to continue with a hand gesture.

Convict mad a slight frown as if to say *are you sure?* Cam nodded and went on with all the details of the meeting.

"Sosa will personally be at the meet," he smiled.

"Along with a hundred kilos of pure cocaine," Cam spelled out as Anthony mentally took notes. He remained mute until Convict excused himself.

"Thanks, Unc. I'ma get a promotion for sure!" the young cop cheered.

"But, where did you hear it from?" Cam reminded.

"My confidential informants that I developed in the streets," he recited just as he'd been taught. Not only did it keep Cam out of the mix but a cop with resources like that was valuable. No doubt he would make detective.

"Good. Very good," Cam nodded with satisfaction. If only things could go that easily with Convict.

****

"Say what?" Convict practically screeched when Cam gave him the change of plans. "You want me to give one-and-a-half-mil to the same nigga that just crossed his partner out? Bruh!"

"Hell naw! We ain't giving him no one-point-five! I got fifty bands that look like a mil," Cam said and opened the bag. The real cash mixed in with the fake cash looked like the million-and-a-half it was supposed to be.

"So... So... So, what 'bout, what 'bout the coke?" Convict asked with greed running down his chin like drool.

"Bruh, let it go. Besides, once Sosa is out of the way, you'll have the streets to yourself."

"Myself? What you mean?" Convict frowned again.

"It means I'm out! Done! The rest of the work is yours!"

"So, I gotta pay like a royalty? Fifty-fifty? That's what's up! I don't mind at all. I..."

"Nah, it's all yours, bruh. I'm good; gonna quit while I'm ahead," he decided. He had been made up his mind but saying it out loud made it final. Greed can make you rich or dead, so it was time to quit while he was ahead.

In truth, Cameron Forrest, AKA Charles Mercer, was way ahead. Not only did he have millions in the bank but he owned the hottest club in the city. His city. More importantly, he had his family. All of his children and a wife to hold him down. You can't put a price on that. It's every dope boy's dream, they just don't know it.

****

"You for real?" Van asked skeptically. "You want me to handle the buy for a hun'ed bricks? A million-and-something dollars?"

"Not if you don't think you can handle it, bruh," Convict said in a condescending tone. "I got this PTA thing at my kid's school. Guess, I'll have to cancel it."

"Nah, nah, I got it. I got it. I done shopped with them before with Havoc before he died," he said as if he wasn't the one who'd killed him. He was still acting from his friend's funeral.

"Okay, cool. Hit me up when you get done," he said and extended his hand. Van was so confused by everything that was going on that he cocked his head curiously at the hand. "Use my car."

"Oh yeah!" he exclaimed when it came to him. He reached out and shook it. Both men knew it would be the last time they saw each other. Van had family down in Florida and planned to take the coke down there and flip it on his own.

Van let out a grunt when he picked up the heavy bag of money. He walked briskly to his car hoping Convict didn't change his mind. He didn't even realize that he was holding his breath until he ran out of breath. He still didn't take one until he pulled away. The bag on the passenger's seat kept nagging at him until he gave in and opened it.

"Oh wow!" he gasped and swerved at the sight of all the money His dick got so hard so fast that he was momentarily blinded. Oddly, he heard his grandmother's voice ring in his ears.

"A bird in the hand beats two in the bush," she advised.

"Fuck that mean, Granny?" he fussed. He gave up on trying to figure it out and called down to Florida. "Granny?"

"Yes, baby?" his grandma smiled. "How you doing, son?"

"Fine, fine. Granny, what did you mean when you used to say that saying 'bout the birds? About the bushes and shit?" he demanded. He didn't mean to be so curt, but he was almost at the motel where the meet was.

"Well, it means be content with what you have. Don't risk a sure thing for something that ain't so sure," she said just as he pulled into the parking lot.

"Look alive! The Benz just pulled in," the lead cop announced as Van pulled in. Then, to everyone's surprise, he busted a U-turn and pulled back out.

"Should we follow him?" a confused cop asked.

"No, Sosa's inside with the dope!" he replied since two Latin men had been seen hauling bags into the room. "Everyone move on the room! Now!"

"I'm on my way down there," Van said as he left the motel because if one bird was better than two, then this mil-and-a-half was better than a hundred kilos of coke. Too bad the mil was only fifty grand. Still, it beat being in that motel room when the cops went rushing in.

"Police!" the police shouted, tossing stun and flash grenades in as they breached the door The two men inside had a split second to decide if they should fight or give up. Both chose life and followed the commands. "Get down! Hands up!"

"Fuck! Can't trust none of these fucking Americans!" Sosa fumed as once again he watched the raid from the safety of his home via security cameras.

Once again, he'd gotten away.

Chapter 33

A wise man knows when to give up as well as when to say fuck this shit and move on. Sosa was a wise man, so that's exactly what he did.

"Fuck this shit!" he fussed and made a call to his private pilot to get his private jet ready.

The police had hit the stash house, which meant Carlos was snitching. It was time to jump ship and go home to his villa.

Sosa was a freak and his biggest regret was not being able to recruit some freaky American freaks to take home with him. He would have to find another way to stock his pond.

Cam waited outside of Sosa's house with an AK-47 for days. He could have waited a month because Sosa wasn't there. He'd wisely retreated to an unknown spot when Carlos got busted with the hundred kilos.

"Fucking Americans," Sosa griped as he drove himself to a Charlie Brown airport in Atlanta. He assumed correctly that his picture would be posted in Hartsfield International. He let out a chuckle of relief when he reached the G-4 on the runway. "Dummies!"

"Welcome aboard, Mr. Sosa," a very pretty black woman smiled. She led the way onto the plane and guided him to his seat.

"Well, hello!" he flirted and checked out her caramel legs and round ass. The short, curly hair framed her lovely face perfectly. The tight stewardess skirt showed off her assets quite nicely.

"Buckle up for take-off," she purred and leaned over him to let him look down her shirt at the plump, softball sized breasts inside.

"You're quite beautiful. I may have a job for you in Brazil. Once we reach cruising altitude, I'll let you try out," he said smugly, as if he was doing her a favor

"Sounds like a plan," she said, licking her lips seductively. "I'll be back once we're airborne. Guess I'll go slip into something a little more comfortable."

"Hey!" Sosa called out just as she reached her section. "I didn't get your name."

"Yolo," she said, flashing that smile before drawing the curtain.

The pilot mashed the gas and lifted the plan off the runway. Meanwhile, Yolo quickly changed into something a little more comfortable before opening the door to the cockpit.

"Does this thing have autopilot?" she asked curiously.

"Sure, just set it," he said.

"Okay, bye-bye," she smiled and shot him in his face.

"What the hell was that?" Sosa demanded as Yolo came back to where he was seated. His next question was, "What the hell are you wearing?"

"A gun shot," she answered and shoved him the gun. "And this is a parachute."

The GPS on Yolo's watch began to beep more rapidly as the rendezvous point approached. When it became steady, she opened the side door. She blew Sosa a kiss and jumped out.

"What the fuck!" Sosa shouted in shock. He ran to the cockpit and found the pilot splattered all over his instruments. He came back out and looked around desperately. A smile spread on his face when he spotted a second parachute.

Sosa plotted his revenge on whoever'd planned this failed assassination attempt as he donned the parachute. He went to open the door and watched as Yolo landed in a field.

He had to wait a moment until they flew past some trees. When he saw the next clearing, he leapt out.

"Don't you know Sosa is an expert skydiver?!" he laughed as he free-fell from the plane. When the distance was right, he pulled the cord.

This would have worked out great had there been a parachute inside. There wasn't, but the cord was connected to ten pounds of plastic explosives.

"Yay!" Yolo cheered at the human fireworks display. Sosa sprinkled form the sky like confetti.

Killa shook his head at his goofy girlfriend and made a call.

"Sup, shawty?" Cam sighed. The frustration of the futile stake out was evident in his voice.

"Done deal, cuz. That's the end of Sosa!" Killa replied.

"The end of the dope boy, too," Cam smiled. He terminated the call and went home to his family. Went home where he belonged.

The End

Family Drama
Chapter 1

Madison scrunched her pretty face up as the strangest feeling began to creep through her body. She momentarily ignored her internal guest as she tried to put a finger on the feeling. It was like someone was speaking a foreign language, yet she could still understand and relate to what was being said. The feeling was part electric and slightly eclectic and a whole lot of wonderful. It seemed to keep building in intensity until she felt like she might explode. Then, she did.

"Shit!" the usually reserved, prim and proper woman shouted as a violent orgasm wracked her body. It was the first of her life, despite having being married almost all of her adult life. Her husband was one of those selfish lovers who was only concerned with his own pleasure.

"Mmmm... I'm right behind you," he said from deep within her body. He had only confirmed what his body was saying. His smooth stroke had started out as withdraw eight inches, slide in nine inches. Now it was choppy and his breath had grown ragged.

Madison spread her smooth, dark chocolate thighs to give up every nook and cranny of her creamy, wet vagina, causing his stokes to increase until he was literally slamming in and out of her, treating her sophisticated vagina like a plain ole pussy.

She would have been embarrassed by the loud squishing and squelching coming from between her legs if not for the fact that she was about to cum again. After forty-five years of life, with twenty-three of them being married, with no orgasm, two in one night was more than she could have ever hoped for.

"Ugh!" came the grunt when he came. He used his feet to push himself all the way against her cervix as he exploded. The ribbed, lubricated condom was put to the test as he pumped it full of semen.

"Shit, shit, shit!" Madison reiterated as she came once more. She almost sounded angry at the orgasm that tore through her, but if busting a nut was wrong, she didn't want to be right.

This was the first time both Mr. and Mrs. Broadnax had ever cum at the same time.

Too bad that they were on opposite sides of town.

****

"Grrr, grrrr, whew!" Paul Broadnax grunted and growled in delight. Tamika tossed her limber legs on his shoulders and thrusted her hips up at him. She squeezed her young vagina around his shaft and milked him dry. Actually, it was a coochie since it was open to the public.

"That's right, baby, cum in this pussy! This your pussy!" she coaxed while rubbing his back. She wasn't lying about it being his because at that precise moment, it was. She said a silent prayer that this would be the dose of semen that knocked her up.

Being a wealthy man's baby's mama was like winning the hood lottery. It sure as hell beat stripping in one of Atlanta's gentlemen's club. Her friend Diamond got a condo, a car and a generous monthly allowance for her bastard son. Now that's a come up.

"Mm-mm-mm," Paul moaned as he dragged his deflating dick around inside of her. He really appreciated her getting on birth control so that he could really feel her good twenty-two-year-old coochie. After twenty-three years of marriage, he preferred raw sex to the muted sensation of a condom. He would have appreciated it even more if her being on it was true.

"Let me up," Tamika said as she rolled out from under him. She rushed into the bathroom and returned in a flash with a warm, soapy washcloth. Paul knew the drill so he laid back to have his package cleaned. She scrubbed their sexual secretions from his dick and balls almost royally.

"Can I go to the D-Lite concert next week?" she purred as she worked.

Paul's mind flashed to his daughter Courtney, who had asked him the same question earlier. Madison and Courtney were close in age but were nothing alike. While Madison worked at the strip club, his daughter was on her way to college. He and the Mrs. had raised their children in upscale suburbs, not inner city squalor. Neither girl was really asking for permission to go, but money to go.

"How much?" he sighed knowingly. He had replied the same way to Courtney, who in turn insisted that it took five-hundred-dollars to get the full experience. He didn't mind paying for VIP rather than having his daughter mingle with common folk.

"Um..." Tamika stalled while checking to make sure his dick was spotless. It was, so she gave it a kiss and felt it began to stiffen once again. She wanted five-hundred-dollars and had no problem sucking a dick to get it. She had sucked plenty of dicks for a lot less. "Five...hun...red."

"Mmm...sure," he agreed as he watched himself disappear into her mouth. You can get more flies with sugar and this was the same principal.

"Muah," she said, kissing on the head of his dick. "I need... 'Muah'...a rental... 'Muah'...a dress... 'Muah'..."

"Better make it a grand just in case," he surmised since he didn't have much more time out. He used her ponytail as a handle to guide her head up and down as he aimed his penis at her tonsils. She gagged slightly at the inevitable eruption but hung in there and swallowed in gulps.

Both the mister and mistress were relieved that it would be an early night. Both had their own reasons for wanting to depart. They were on the same page but definitely different paragraphs.

Tamika planned to hit the club to shake her money maker for more money. Despite her box being full of semen, she hadn't ruled out fucking but if she did, they would have to use a condom.

Paul, on the other hand, had to get home to his wife, who had been grumbling about his all-nighters. The complaining had abruptly stopped, which made him take heed, but it was 'too little, too late'.

****

When a woman's fed up, she gives up. It had taken decades of being treated like a maid, a nanny and a sex slave for Madison to get here. 'Here' was a hotel on the outskirts of town with her skirt off and a young man between her thighs sucking her vagina.

She'd paid a pretty penny for the pretty boy, but he was eating her out for free. As a matter of fact, her vagina was so pretty, so clean and so tight that he would've paid her to eat it.

She came with a gush of fluid that filled his mouth and that was payment enough.

"I h-h-h-ha-have t-t-t-to go," Madison managed to stutter.

Had he said 'No, stay here forever', she might have. His company in the hotel room sure beat being alone in the mini mansion she called home.

Although four people called the five-thousand-square-foot house home, it seemed as if she was the only one who lived there. Her son Brandon was away at college in downtown Atlanta, which he obviously thought was too far away to visit his mom. Her daughter Courtney technically lived there but rarely graced the place with her face. She made NASCAR worthy pit stops to change clothes or get money for clothes, but other than that, senior year activities kept her busy. In a few months, she too would be off to college. Then she would really be alone, despite being married.

"Excuse me, ma'am," the young man said, waving his hand to extract her from her own thoughts.

"Yes?" she replied politely even though she could do without the *ma'am*. She knew he was young enough to be her child, no need to rub it in.

"Anytime you need to hook up, just let me know," he said as he prepared to leave.

"I know where to find you...yes," she said, forgetting his name. She had it until he made her cum so hard. It had that Etch-a-Sketch effect, wiping her memory clean. She knew it was on the website she'd found him on and since she planned on visiting again, she left it alone.

"Okay, thanks again!" he said, flashing that smile that made him a final contestant when she browsed the 'college hunk' website.

"No, thank you," she replied because she was polite and he made her cum for the first time in her life. Although it was the first time, it wouldn't be the last.